WISH UPON A STAR

Abandoning her life and starting anew seemed like the best option for Claire. Now, seven years on, she is helping to run a successful nightclub in Newcastle, and her daughter Gemma, boss Lee and his wife Cari are all the family she needs. The last person she expects to see is her ex — who just happens to be rock star Mark Crofts. No one has ever taken Claire's place in his heart. But can he win her back?

CHARLOTTE McFALL

---◆---

WISH UPON A STAR

Complete and Unabridged

LINFORD
Leicester

First published in Great Britain in 2012

First Linford Edition
published 2017

A catalogue record for this book is available
from the British Library.

ISBN 978–1–4448–3474–1

Published by
F. A. Thorpe (Publishing)
Anstey, Leicestershire

Set by Words & Graphics Ltd.
Anstey, Leicestershire
Printed and bound in Great Britain by
T. J. International Ltd., Padstow, Cornwall

This book is printed on acid-free paper

1

Claire cast one final glance over the interior of the newly-opened nightclub and nodded her approval.

'You're looking pleased with yourself,' a gruff voice noted from behind her on the upper balcony.

Claire glanced over her shoulder and grinned at the gentleman who joined her. 'Just enjoying the view, Lee. I'm so glad we're finally open.'

Lee McGuire, the owner of a successful chain of nightclubs in the north of the country, nodded in agreement with Claire. As his assistant, and publicity manager for his latest venture, she had worked with him from day one on the ideas and designs for Stars, the biggest nightclub in Newcastle. After eighteen months of planning and hard work, the club had opened two nights before to rave reviews from local and national press.

'Well, you've got every right to be proud. I couldn't have done it without you, Claire.' Lee smiled warmly at the woman who had come to his door seven years before, looking for part-time bar work. The same woman he now looked upon as the daughter he and his wife, Cari, had never had.

The club was set on two floors, with a bar and dance floor on each, and a balcony running around the top level, where Claire and Lee were currently standing. Above them, the ceiling glowed with a million tiny stars which faded down the midnight-blue walls onto the lower level, until there was nothing but the odd star glinting on the floor.

From the outset of the project, Lee had relied heavily on Claire for ideas and valued her opinions greatly. She had worked her way up from barmaid, to bar manager, to his publicity manager in a matter of years.

'You look tired. You shouldn't be

working so hard.'

'That's rich, Lee!' Claire smiled. 'Who was it that phoned me at seven-thirty this morning begging me to come in early just to go over tonight's proceedings with you?'

'I needed you to oversee every minute detail.'

'Yeah, everything except tonight's mystery guest!' Claire exclaimed. 'Who is it, Lee? Royalty?'

'As good as! Still, everything's ready now.'

'Just as well — it's about time I picked up my daughter. Good luck for tonight, Lee. Not that you'll need it.' She kissed him on the cheek. 'I'll see you bright and early tomorrow morning.'

Lee's voice stopped her in her tracks. 'I need you here tonight.'

'What for? All the systems are working; there's more than enough bar cover, so you won't end up pulling pints like we did on opening night.' She stuck her hands on her jean-clad hips, her lips pursed.

Lee thought quickly. She *had* organised everything so that it ran like clockwork. There was no doubt in his mind that she was the best thing that had happened to his business. Claire's even temper and everlasting patience acted as counterbalance to his messiness and extremely short fuse.

'I need you to act as my hostess.'

'What? Lee, I'm leaving now. It's eight o'clock. I've been here for nearly twelve hours. I haven't even seen daylight. All I really want to do is to go home and relax.'

'You need some fun, Claire. When was the last time you had a night out? See, you can't remember!' he crowed triumphantly. 'I've already discussed it with Cari. She's more than happy to have Gemma stay the night.'

'And what did Gemma say? As if I need to ask.' Claire felt as if she was being backed into a corner and could see no chance for escape. 'I have nothing to wear!' She indicated her jeans and tee shirt in a futile, last-ditch attempt to flee.

'We've thought of that one!' Lee winked at her, before disappearing through the staff door to the offices.

'It's a conspiracy,' she muttered a moment later, as Lee handed her a garment bag. Inside she found a black cocktail dress and recognised it immediately. She had tried it on for a laugh a few days ago whilst shopping with Cari. She glanced from the dress to Lee, and back, and saw the expectant look on his kind face.

Claire knew that he had been puzzled and a little hurt at her stubborn reluctance to participate in the opening night celebrations, either as a hostess or as a guest. Claire wished she could give Lee the real reason why she did not wish to mingle with the rich and famous guests. She knew that it would sound strange to someone who doted on public attention.

Claire was no stranger to the spotlight. Her mother was a leading novelist, her sister a model. Just before Claire's sixteenth birthday, her father had died, leaving her devastated. He had been her rock, giving her life a sense of normality. With him gone, her world had seemed to close in on her as the media attention increased. The one person who had loved her for who she was had gone, and she had vowed never to let anyone close to her, to let them see how vulnerable she was.

Claire shivered unconsciously at the thought of being under that intense scrutiny and realised that Lee was still waiting for her answer.

'I don't appear to have much choice,' she said quietly.

'You will always have a choice, Claire.' Lee's tone was kindly, but she knew that it would mean a lot to him if she stayed. He wanted her to share in his glory, and it was the least she could do for the man who had looked out for her all these years.

'I'll stay.' Her heart warmed to see a smile light up his face. 'It'll be fun, and besides, you're right. I haven't been out much lately.' Lee grinned as she hugged him. 'The dress is beautiful, by the way. Thank you.'

★ ★ ★

'And we're off the air!' The floor manager announced, as the red light on camera four went out.

Everyone began to bustle around, hurrying to clear the set. Mark let the smile fade from his face, his jaw aching from maintaining it for so long for the cameras. The talk show host shooed away his assistants as he stood up and extended his hand to Mark.

'Mark! You have a really good relationship with the camera. Ever thought of branching out into the acting business?' David Williams smiled.

Mark released the man's hand with a brief shake of his dark head. 'I don't need any more work at the moment, David.'

'That's right. You're off on holiday,

7

aren't you?' David's glance flickered to the notes on Mark that he had referred to throughout the interview. 'Any special plans?'

'No.' Mark was no longer forthcoming now the cameras were off.

The chance for further probing by the interviewer was cut short by the arrival of Mark's manager, Justin Lloyd-Smith. Justin had been with Mark since the formation of his band, Equinox, which had become one of the biggest groups in Europe. In time, Mark had left the band, with Justin following, and together they had cornered the market on both sides of the Atlantic. Mark was one of the biggest selling solo artists of the year.

'Brilliant, Mark.' Justin slapped him on the back. 'You gave them exactly what they wanted, a glimpse of the real Mark Crofts.'

Mark smiled half-heartedly. He desperately needed some time off. He'd been suffering for weeks with lingering symptoms of 'flu, but the holiday he was about to take was as much for his mental health as for his physical health. He needed to sort out his thoughts, make some sense of the last few years.

He had been to see his family doctor. Mark hadn't been to the area in the last couple of years, and he had suddenly felt the need to touch base. Even though his parents had long since moved away, he still thought of it as home.

Mark had been in the surgery less than five minutes when Doctor Franklin delivered his diagnosis.

'You're on the verge of physical exhaustion, Mark. Your body is tired. You need to take a long break.'

This was indeed true. Many nights, he awoke from sleep in a cold sweat, left with an image of a dream that was so vivid it felt like it had been burned into his eyelids. Every time he closed his eyes, he could see the face of the woman he had once loved, the woman he had believed loved him. But her disappearance one night had told him otherwise. Now, all he had were feelings of regret.

So why then, should he be dreaming of her after all these years? These dreams were dark and brooding, totally the opposite of how he actually remembered her. The only darkness about her was her chestnut hair, shot through with auburn, so that at times it seemed as if she was made of liquid fire. Her eyes were the colour of a star-filled sky. In his dreams, however, there were no stars. It was as if all light had died in her, and he had been left in darkness.

The remembrance of her was with him in his waking hours also. He would see a beautiful woman with long dark curls and his heartbeat would begin to race. He would find himself staring at her intently, willing her to turn around and be his lost love. But she never was.

* * *

Mark blinked as a brightly-lit lamp was wheeled past him by a stagehand, as the set was cleared for the next program.

'Are you ready to leave?' Justin put a friendly arm around Mark's shoulders.

'Yes. Let's go. I've had enough of this place.'

They stepped out of the building, and a sense of freedom spread through Mark's entire body as he inhaled the crisp air deeply. Justin seemed to be in more of a hurry, mainly to escape the attention of the groups of female fans gathered outside the studios. He practically pushed Mark into the waiting black limousine.

'Thank God that's over,' Justin sighed, pushing his dark glasses up onto his head.

Mark tuned out the sound of Justin's voice, and looked out of the tinted window. The car passed city block after city block, grey upon grey, as they were driven back to the record company offices. He reminded himself that the next day he would be surrounded by open spaces and green countryside and normal, genuine people. He was sick to death of hearing false sincerity wherever he went from the people he dealt with every day. He needed to distance himself for a while from the business that had consumed his life for so long.

For many years, fawning people had surrounded him in the music business. Everything was to do with image and publicity, and nothing to do with real people at all. Maybe, Mark thought, that was why he was dreaming of her so much. It felt as if the last time he had been real to someone had been when she had shared his life. She seemed to have been the last honest and sincere person Mark had known, and with her departure, all things real had gone too.

Mark had been so disillusioned with life when she left him that he had stopped trying to see the best in people — something she had taught him — and filled his life with fast living, fast cars and all the trappings that wealth and fame brought. So why now, after all these years of stardom, did he feel so incomplete? Was it that when he was home at night, alone, with no adoring fans and no cameras flashing in his face, he was left with an empty shell? Or was it that he simply did not exist anymore, that when she left, she had taken the real Mark with her?

'I need you to do me a favour.'

'What?' Mark's tone was wary as he flicked Justin a look.

'One more appearance?' The request hung in the air for a long moment, and Justin appeared to shrink back into the seat.

'Damn it, Justin!' Mark exclaimed, his tone impatient. 'I told you that interview was the last thing I wanted to do. I need this holiday!'

'It's for an old friend of mine.' The whine in Justin's voice set Mark's nerves on edge.

'Who is it?'

'Lee McGuire. He started out as a cabaret act in the sixties, and worked his way up through the club circuit. He has a couple of nightclubs up north. He's just opened up his third.'

'Is he small-time?'

'Sure. The only reason I asked is because you're going up that end of the country anyway. It's in Newcastle.'

'The only reason — apart from me saving your hide, perhaps? Do you owe him money?' Mark knew that Justin was a gambler.

'I lost to him in a card game last month. So I sort of used you as an I.O.U.' Justin at least had the grace to look sheepish.

Mark had to smile. 'You are so back-handed!'

'You'll do it?'

'Give me the details.' He had long been resigned to the fact that his personal life was destined to take a back seat to his career for as long as he was in the spotlight, but that fact now bothered the hell out of him.

Justin handed him an itinerary that had him on a plane to Newcastle that afternoon to arrive at the club about nine o'clock that evening, and a flight to Edinburgh the next morning.

'It's the last time I bail you out, Justin.'

Justin grinned happily, and Mark wished he could please himself as easily.

*   *   *

'This is the place.'

Mark leaned forward to look out of the tinted front window, and frowned. 'Are you sure?' he asked the chauffeur. There were hundreds of people gathered outside the building.

'Yes, sir. The place just opened two days ago. Biggest nightclub in the North East.'

Mark cast a glance at the beautiful woman who was seated beside him, re-touching her make-up. Noticing his perusal, she flashed him a smile.

'I'm ready, Mark!' She placed a hand on his thigh and squeezed it gently. Jennifer was a model with whom Mark had been romantically linked by the press. Justin had seen their coupling as a good publicity stunt and so Mark had taken her out a few times.

The car door opened and Mark saw a tall, well-built man, leaning towards him to help him from the car. He took the extended hand and registered a faint feeling of reassurance in the firmness of the handshake.

'Lee McGuire. Thank you very much for agreeing to do this tonight.' Lee's eyes were sparkling as camera flashes popped in his face from every angle.

'Nice to meet you, Lee. Looks like you've got a popular place here!' Mark helped Jennifer out of the car, and whilst Lee introduced himself to her, Mark looked around him properly for the first time and was quite amazed by the sheer number of people.

'Please, come inside.' And so saying, Lee took Jennifer's arm and led her up the steps to the door with Mark by her side, giving them a potted history of the building on the way.

The crowds seemed to be cheering louder with every step Mark took. The smile on his handsome face faltered a few times in the seemingly eternal walk from car to entrance. Mark could feel his head pounding, his adrenaline running at high pitch. Then, just as soon as it had started, the noise and commotion were over, as they came to a halt in the midnight-blue foyer.

Following Lee up a flight of stairs, not participating in the conversation he and Jennifer were engaged in, Mark began to think that maybe it was not going to be such a bad night. Perhaps it would be just a couple of hours, as Justin had promised him. The bouncers had not let in a single member of the paparazzi, and there had been no sign of any press in the foyer.

Upon entering the room, Mark could not see for the cameras and the people pressing to get a better look at him. He felt frustration rise in him again, his face passive and a smile frozen there, but inside he was seething.

Across the bar, Claire's conversation with the head bartender was inter-rupted by a sudden mêlée, and she

17

turned to see what the commotion was all about. She could just about make out Lee's smiling face above the heads of the guests that were assembled, but the general fuss and the flashing of the camera bulbs eclipsed all sight of the people at Lee's side. Lee raised his hand in greeting to Claire, and she waved back before turning back to her conversation partner.

'Here we go!' She rolled her eyes, making Patrick, the bar manager, laugh. Claire watched him give brief orders to his staff, and then she felt a tap on her shoulder. With a smile, she turned around.

'Claire, this is Mark Crofts and Jennifer Munroe. Claire Montague, my publicity manager,' said Lee, watching Claire's face triumphantly as he made the introductions to see if she was impressed.

Claire hardly heard his words, bombarded as she was with a thousand thoughts all at once. As she looked into the eyes of this man, this star, who stood in front of her, all she could think about was the last time she had seen him. Here was the very man she had spent much of the last seven years trying to forget, suppressing memories, hopes and dreams. A breath shuddered from her throat, as if Mark had reached inside and dragged it from her.

Mark heard Lee talking about Claire, but he could only look silently at her, as if he could not quite believe that she was standing before him after so long. His dark eyes flitted over her slim body, sheathed in an expensive dress, the black silk clinging to the curves that he had once known intimately. Her dark chestnut hair glowed with hidden fire, the smooth skin of her cheeks echoing that heat as she coloured, but Claire was watching him with ice in her eyes, and he could imagine that ice spreading all over her body if he came any nearer.

Lee, having finished the introductions, was waiting for Claire to say something. She extended her hand, bracing herself for Mark's touch.

Mark had been expecting her skin to be cool to the touch, to match the air that she was giving off, but her skin was as warm and smooth as he remembered it. Every nerve ending in Mark's body seemed to be teased by fire at her touch; his reaction was instantly cooled with the icy stare she fixed him with.

Claire herself felt Jennifer's glare upon her. Her intense scrutiny, combined with Mark's stare, was too much. Turning abruptly to Lee, she blurted, 'I'm needed elsewhere.'

Without a second glance, Claire turned her back on the group and walked away. Mark watched Claire's retreating figure.

'She's obviously star struck.' Jennifer's voice filtered into Mark's thoughts. 'She isn't used to meeting famous people, I expect.'

'How do you know?' Mark snapped at her.

Jennifer frowned. 'I could tell. She couldn't keep her eyes off you.' There was an edge to her voice that grated on Mark's nerves.

'How about I introduce you to some friends?' Lee interjected, and his two guests put aside their discussion and followed their host.

Claire felt her world held no sense of reality anymore. She uttered a small cry of desperation as she rushed out of the bar, stumbling down the stairs to her office. All the way, she felt as if the walls were closing in around her. She practically ran the last few steps into her office, shutting the door firmly behind her, as if the action could keep out the sensations she felt.

She was knocked sideways as emotions came flooding back in a tide that overwhelmed her completely. The mere sight of Mark's face had acted as a conduit to a past that she truly believed she had dealt with. She had loved him once, deeply and completely, but Mark had hurt her more than she had words to describe, and for the longest time, she had harboured feelings of hate and disgust for him. Over the years, she came to view the circumstances of their relationship with a tempered manner, and she knew that it was for the best that she had left him.

Time, and Gemma, had made Claire moderate in her dealings with people, and she realised that her memories had overridden her common sense when she had come face to face with Mark. It was a shock, to say the least, but much worse was the possibility of Mark finding out the secret she had kept for years.

Suddenly, she felt nauseous. There was no way she could stay here, not while Mark was in the same building. Just the thought of him was enough to throw her into confusion again. She'd pick up Gemma and go home, where she was safe, just as she should have done all along. For now, for her own sanity, she had to get away from Mark.

Mark was sitting at the bar, nursing a whiskey to calm his mind. He was shaking.

'Enjoying yourself?' Jennifer purred in his ear, her hand on his shoulder.

'So-so. How about you?'

'I'd be better if I had some company.'

Jennifer had not bothered to ask why he was seated alone at the bar. Someone else might have inquired if he were feeling all right; someone who cared for him. But there was no one like that in his life, there hadn't been since Claire.

'Mark, would you like to walk around with me? At least look like you have some interest?' Her tone was biting, but Mark had already forgotten it as he saw Claire re-enter the bar.

'Let's go,' he said, taking her arm and moving before Jennifer had time to change her mind.

As they mingled, Mark kept a constant eye on Claire, who was looking for Lee. He watched her as she moved around the room, and as she had a conversation with Lee.

'What's wrong?' Lee looked deep into Claire's eyes.

'I told you, Lee, I really can't talk to you now. I promise I'll explain in the morning.'

Something made Claire turn her head to the side, and she found Mark gazing at her. Panicking, she almost wrenched her arm from Lee's grip, her eyes wide. 'I'm sorry!' she whispered, as she took a faltering step backwards before turning on her heel and disappearing through the private door once more.

Mark had an overwhelming urge to go after Claire, to make her talk to him, to answer questions. He didn't, not right then. But a firm resolve settled in the pit of his stomach. He would have those answers from Claire if it killed him, just as it almost had when she walked out of his life before. This time, he was not about to let her disappear.

Driving like she was being pursued by a pack of wolves, instead of her memories of Mark, Claire made it to Cari's house in record time. Her heart was still racing as she climbed out of the car and knocked on the front door. It opened, and Cari stood there.

'Hey, Cari!' Claire muttered, as Cari stood back to allow her to enter. As she closed the door, Claire strained her ears for any sound of her daughter. 'Is Gemma asleep already?'

'No. She's playing on the computer. Do you want me to call her?'

'Um, no. I need something strong to calm my nerves before I have to deal with her.' Claire shivered, and Cari noted her pale face.

'Come into the kitchen. The fire's on. You look like you've seen a ghost.'

Taking a seat at the scrubbed pine table in Cari's kitchen, Claire gazed into the fire. She didn't notice when Cari put a steaming cup of whiskey-laced black coffee in front of her, rousing herself from a Mark-filled reverie when Gemma came skipping into the room.

'Mum!' Her voice penetrated Claire's mind, causing her to look up, blinking her eyes. 'What are you doing here?'

Then, noticing her dress, Gemma smiled. 'You're pretty.'

'Hey, sweetheart! I just thought I'd pop by to say hello. I haven't seen you all day.' Claire smiled, but it looked like an effort to Cari.

'I thought you were acting as Lee's hostess tonight. I just spoke to him, and he sounded really peeved that you walked out on him,' Cari pointed out.

'A job which was dumped on me at the last minute. Thanks for the warning, Cari!' Claire's tone was sharp, and Cari raised an eyebrow. Claire was the most level person she knew, and the acid quality to her voice seemed strange.

'Let's have a little less of the attitude, please?' she rebuked mildly.

Claire sat upright, and looked at Cari. 'What else did Lee say?'

'Just that you met Mark Crofts and ended up bolting the room,' Cari said breezily, loud enough for Gemma to hear. Claire tried to stop her from uttering his name, but too late, for Gemma had looked up with interest at the mention of her idol.

'Your mother met Mark Crofts tonight, darling,' Cari informed the little girl.

'No!' gasped a shocked Gemma. She rounded the table to face Claire. 'You saw him?' Her questioning tone held a modicum of disbelief, but her eyes were shining with hope.

Claire's heart went out to the little girl. She wished she could lie to her, to protect her from disappointment, but Cari had already shot that one down in flames.

'Yes, Gemma, I met him. He was at the club.'

A strange mixture of emotions flickered across Gemma's face before she said, quietly, 'You didn't say. I could've gone too.' Claire shrugged, too tired to explain that if she had known Mark was going to be there, she most certainly wouldn't have been. 'You know I love him!'

'Gemma, you can't love someone you don't know.'

Tears fell in earnest from Gemma's grey eyes, her lower lip trembling violently. She stared at her mother for a long moment. 'I hate you!' were her last words as she raced from the kitchen, doors slamming in her wake.

Claire looked at Cari helplessly.

'Sorry, love.' Cari's voice was quiet as she patted Claire's hand on the table. 'I'll go and talk to her.'

Claire silently contemplated her coffee. She had spent seven long years trying to forget Mark Crofts, and now in less than a few hours, he was back in her life, and coming between her and Gemma. She had lost all control of her rational thoughts and tempered emotions, and also the respect of her daughter, in a few short hours.

Closing her eyes, Claire sat still, until Cari had rejoined her at the table.

'Is she okay?' Claire's eyes were dull as she looked at her friend. 'Does she hate me?'

Cari smiled. 'No, Claire, she doesn't hate you. Don't you remember ever telling your mother that you hated her when the two of you argued? People say all kind of things when they're upset. They don't necessarily mean them.'

'That was all I ever did, argue with my mother. We used to fight like cat and dog.' A sardonic smile flickered around Claire's mouth.

'Did you not get along?'

'We did okay, I suppose, when I was younger. I was closer to my dad, and Mother preferred my sister.'

'That's the first time I've ever heard you mention your family. You never talk about them.'

Claire shrugged. 'Once I moved up here, I didn't really see the point of keeping in touch. Gemma's my family now, and you and Lee.'

'You said you were close to your father. What about him?'

Unwanted tears filled Claire's eyes, and she rubbed at a tiny frown that appeared in her brow. 'Dad, he, uh . . . he died when I was fifteen.'

'Claire, I'm sorry.' Cari was quick to

apologise. The little scene with Gemma, coupled with the strange events of that evening, had had an astounding effect on Claire. Cari could see once again the young girl who had appeared in their lives years before, fragile and confused.

'No, it's okay. I got over it a long time ago. I don't know why I'm crying,' Claire said with a small laugh, wiping away the tears on her cheeks. 'I'm just tired. I should have handled that situation with Gemma better.'

'That was my fault, love.' Cari accepted the blame. 'I didn't realise you didn't want her to know.'

'I don't. I mean, it's not that. Oh God, I don't know what I mean. Everything's so up in the air!' With a sigh, Claire took a gulp of her coffee, and her thoughts began to wander.

'Claire,' Cari started, 'something's shaken you up. It has something to do with this Mark Crofts, doesn't it?'

Claire shrugged. 'I know Mark.'

Cari raised one eyebrow. 'How well did you know him?'

Claire took a deep breath before she answered, 'We were engaged.'

'And you broke up?'

'No, I left him.'

'Why?'

Claire frowned. She shrugged, finding the memory too painful to put into words.

'Tell me how you got involved with Mark.' Cari leaned back in her chair, offering Claire a chance to regain her equilibrium.

'I worked in a record store with Mark. He played in a band in his spare time. He'd play me the songs he had written on his guitar after work, and I'd go to watch him rehearse.' Cari noticed how Claire's voice had softened as she spoke of him. 'We were friends for a year before we became involved.'

'Did you love him?'

'I did.' Claire's words were firm, and Cari contemplated her thoughtfully.

'But you left him.' Cari's statement was innocuous, but it caught Claire up and twisted her heart.

'I found him with another woman,' Claire spat, and shivered, the memory repulsing her.

Cari stayed silent, sorry that she had initiated the conversation. For her part, Claire, wanted to scream out loud, but instead she spoke in a monotone, her eyes glazed.

'I was on my way up to our flat, and I ran into Mark's manager. He told me not to go up, that Mark was busy, but I had some news for him and couldn't wait. When I opened the front door, I saw him sprawled half-naked on the couch with a woman bending over him.' Claire voice cracked slightly, and Cari put her hand over hers. 'I ran back out and tripped over something. The next thing I knew, I woke up in hospital. Mark was in the corner of the room talking to Justin about our wedding. Justin told him that he had to call it off. I waited until they went and I discharged myself. I had to get away.'

'Why didn't you tell us before?' Ever since the young girl had arrived on their doorstep, looking for a job at Lou's Lounge, Cari had always wondered what could have driven her so far from home.

'I just wanted to forget all about it when I first came here, and then after that, Gemma came along, and I just put it out of my mind.'

'Until Mark showed up last night.'

'It just dragged up memories I would rather forget.'

'Are you going to explain any of this to Gemma?'

'No!' was Claire's sharp answer. A frown creased her brow as she picked up her coffee cup and took a big gulp. The bitterness of the dark, black liquid matched the tumultuous racing of her mind as she tried to steady her thoughts. Why was she acting like this? She knew that her reactions to the situation with Mark were extreme, but she could not reconcile herself in her current position as the mother of a six-year-old child with the person her heart was remembering; the person she had been when she had left the man she loved. Taking a deep breath, Claire looked at Cari who was watching her with an intent expression.

'What are you looking at me like that for?'

Cari blinked as if she had been startled. 'I just wondered why you don't want to tell Gemma. She'd be thrilled to know that you were once close to her hero!' There was an edge to Cari's voice that Claire didn't like. She was still looking at her with a question in her eyes.

'It's not that important.'

'Then why not tell her?'

'Leave it, Cari!' Claire's voice was steel-like. Cari was pushing at doors that had been slammed and locked shut years since, and Claire had no intention of taking a crowbar to them now. There was a heavy silence between the two women then, each occupied with her own thoughts. Cari spoke first, causing Claire to startle.

'Are you taking tomorrow off?'

Claire had been thrown off guard by her discussion with Cari, and had not righted herself emotionally. 'What for? Oh damn, teacher training! I'll have to take her into work with me.'

'You're pretty busy at the moment, remember? You know what she's like, she'll be bored. I know you're Super Mum, but . . .'

Claire grinned. 'You wouldn't think it to look at me, would you? I manage to upset my daughter, and waste a perfectly good cocktail dress, all because of some man I haven't seen for years. Super Silly, maybe!'

Cari laughed, rising to pick up the empty coffee cups. 'Leave her here for her sleepover. I'll take her to the circus tomorrow, and then we can all have dinner tomorrow night.'

'Thanks, Cari. That'd be nice.'

Half an hour later, a smiling Gemma kissed her mother warmly goodbye, promising to save her some popcorn and candy floss, waving as Claire started the engine and drove away. A pounding was beginning behind her temples as she drove home, but not wanting to dwell on the cause, she blocked all thoughts from her head.

Once home, Claire reassured herself that she would be fine once she had a good night's sleep. But as she fell asleep, the only thing that filled her mind was the image of Mark, smiling at her as he had once done.

2

Mark was certainly not smiling when he awoke that morning, hungover and too late to catch his flight. The headache he was suffering had started shortly after Claire had left last night, when Mark had started drinking heavily. A blazing row with Jennifer in the limousine on the way back to her hotel had not finished off the evening very well for him.

Having decided to drive to Edinburgh, it was mid-afternoon when Mark set off. Several thoughts jostled for prominence in his mind as he negotiated the traffic in the city centre, and the ones involving Claire won. Mark had been angry at her departure last night for several reasons, one being his pride; how dare she dismiss him like that? Didn't she know that he could have any woman he wanted? He could have taken Jennifer into his bed last night, except for the fact that he could only see Claire as he looked at her.

The memories of her desertion were fresh in his mind. He never discovered where she'd gone, despite repeated searches by the private investigators he had hired. The reason for that, as he thought back to last night, was that she was now called Claire Montague — her mother's maiden name, a possibility that Mark had never even considered.

'Why am I even thinking about her now?' Mark muttered crossly, as a car cut across his path. But he knew why. He wanted answers from seven years ago, and he was scared that she would disappear again. He had to know why she had left him; she owed him that much.

Mark found himself outside Stars. Determined, and without a thought as to whether or not he was permitted to park outside the club, Mark locked the door to the Range Rover, and climbed the steps. As he suspected, the doors were locked from the inside and he could not see through the windows to get anyone's attention. Looking to his left, he found an intercom on the wall next to the doorframe. He pressed the button and waited, pressing it again when no one answered. Finally, there was a buzz of static as a male voice spoke.

'We're closed. If you're a salesman, phone the business office and make an appointment.'

'I'm not a salesman. I'd like to speak to Claire Montague.'

'She's not here.'

'Then I'd like to see Lee McGuire.' Mark did not like the dismissive tone in the man's voice, and a tinge of superiority crept into his own voice.

'And you are?'

'Just tell him it's Mark Crofts.'

There was a brief silence, then the man spoke again.

'Mr. McGuire will be right with you. The door's open.'

Mark entered through the heavy door

into the dark lobby, seeing the security guard disappear through another set of doors. Whilst he waited for Lee, Mark scanned the glossy posters on the wall advertising future appearances, and he was impressed with the calibre of the famous guests that would be attending.

'Mark!' Lee's deep voice rumbled across the foyer. Mark turned with a smile and accepted Lee's extended hand. 'This is a surprise. It's good to see you. It was a real pleasure having you here last night. I mean that sincerely, plus the fact that the cashier's receipts were almost up a hundred percent from our opening night!'

Mark merely acknowledged Lee's compliment with a slight smile. 'I was just looking at all the guests you have lined up for the next month.'

Lee beckoned Mark to follow him, and spoke as they walked through to the office suite. 'All credit goes to Claire. She's done a marvellous job of taking care of the publicity.' With a glance at Mark, he continued, 'She's normally here in the daytime, but she begged off this morning.'

Mark showed no emotion on his face as he replied, 'I was just passing, and thought I'd look in on her. I haven't seen her for a few years.'

'Yes, I heard that.' Lee paused to punch in a code on the security door to the offices he and Claire occupied, allowing Mark to pass through. 'She'll be here later though. She has a meeting with our brewery representative at seven.'

'I doubt I'll still be here then.' His tone told Lee that Mark was not used to being kept waiting, but he quickly qualified the statement. 'I'm going on holiday for a couple of weeks, so I wanted to be on my way by later this afternoon.'

'Anywhere exotic?'

'Just Scotland. My doctor told me I needed a break, so I opted for somewhere peaceful.'

'It must get really hectic for you at times, what with all the appearances!'

Lee winked, as Mark glanced at him with a smile.

'I must admit that I was reluctant to come here last night, but Justin begged.'

'Ah, yes, Justin. Has he been with you long?'

'About nine years. How do you know him?'

Lee laughed heartily at Mark's comment. 'Please, sit down.' He offered Mark a seat on the royal blue sofa, seating himself in an over-stuffed leather armchair that had been his favourite for years. 'Justin and I go way back. When I first settled in Newcastle, I had a talent agency, and Justin worked for me. Over the years, we kept in touch, playing poker every now and then. The last time I saw him, he was boasting about how well he had done for himself and offered you as collateral when he ran out of money. I took him up on the offer. I hope you don't mind?'

'Not at all. Besides, I met Claire again. That was a surprise.'

'For her, too.'

'Is that what she said?' Mark leaned forward, resting his forearms on his knees.

'That's what Claire told my wife. We didn't even know she knew you. She's never been one for opening up.'

'Really? She was always open when I knew her.'

Lee shrugged. 'People change.'

'I guess,' Mark said quietly.

A noise at the door to the office caused both men to look up as Cari and Gemma entered without knocking.

'Grandpa Lee!' Gemma charged across the room and into Lee's open arms. 'I haven't seen you for ages!'

Cari followed, smiling and dropped a kiss on her husband's balding head.

'It's been all of two days, sweetheart!' Lee smiled, as he met Mark's amused eyes over Gemma's dark head of curls.

'It's ages,' she announced dramatically, rolling her eyes. 'I had school all week, but today we didn't. Nana Cari took me to the circus. There's lions and elephants, and clowns. It was brilliant!' Gemma's animated description of the morning's events caused Lee to look at Mark again, and Gemma suddenly noticed that there was someone else in the room. Turning, she said politely, 'I'm sorry.'

But as soon as she saw who was sitting just a few feet away from her, the good manners and breeding that had been taught to her by her mother flew right out of the window.

'Damn!' she exclaimed, her eyes wide and shining. Mark looked at her with a smile. She looked decidedly familiar, but he could not place her.

'Gemma! What have I told you about your language?' Cari interjected sternly.

'Mum says it! Wow!' Then she was suddenly dumbstruck to find Mark staring back at her levelly, and turned, blushing, to hide in Lee's arms. Lee and Cari laughed.

'Mark, this is Gemma. She is your biggest fan. Say hello!' Lee pushed her slightly, but she held on tight to the man who had been her grandpa for her whole life. Shyly, she shook her head, but sneaked a peek at her idol.

'Don't be silly, love!' Cari ruffled her hair. Holding out her other hand, she said, 'Hello, Mark. I'm Cari, Lee's wife.'

'Pleased to meet you, Cari. Who is this young lady?'

'Gemma is Claire's daughter,' Lee informed him, and neither he nor Cari missed the expression of pure surprise on Mark's face.

'Claire's?' The tone of disbelief had a decided effect on Gemma, and she turned to face Mark squarely. The fact that she only had a single parent made her very defensive of her mother.

'I'm Gemma Montague, and Claire's my mummy.' Her little outburst was softened however, by her lovely smile. 'Pleased to meet you, Mr. Crofts.'

'Call me Mark,' he offered softly, as he bent down to get a good look at her. Gemma blushed, and Mark couldn't help but remember when Claire used to do that. 'So, you're Claire's girl,' he whispered.

'She's just like her mother,' Cari put in, watching him closely. There seemed to be so much emotion in those thunder-grey eyes of his, and it had something to do with Gemma, from the way Mark was studying her little face. Cari remembered Claire's reluctance to inform her daughter of her previous acquaintance with Mark. Yes, Mark had hurt Claire, but what did that have to do with Gemma. And yet, looking at the pair of them together . . .

'Just like her mother,' Mark murmured in agreement. 'How old are you, Gemma?'

'Six.'

'I bet your mum is really proud of you.'

Gemma shrugged coyly, causing Mark to smile.

'Gemma was very put out when she found out that Claire met you last night,' Cari informed Mark, her mind racing as she made the connection between Mark and Gemma. 'She has all your albums, don't you, love?'

'Yes, and posters. And Mum says I might go to one of your concerts when I'm big.'

'Would your mum come with you?'

A thoughtful look crossed Gemma's face, and Mark felt an odd tug at his heartstrings. Looking at the little girl reminded him so much of the Claire he had known long ago, and the memory filled him with a sense of loss.

'I don't know,' was Gemma's honest answer.

As Cari and Gemma left the room to fetch coffee for everyone, questions crowded Mark's mind; was Claire with anyone, and, if so, was this man Gemma's father? It hadn't occurred to him, as he had climbed the steps to the club, that Claire had made a life for herself without him, had borne a daughter to someone.

Gemma reminded Mark so much of Claire that after he had finished his coffee, he felt himself becoming extremely agitated. He made his excuses to leave, armed with a phone number where he could reach Claire, and with good wishes from Lee and Cari.

When Claire arrived at the club just before seven, Lee had already left, to take Cari and Gemma to dinner. It was probably just as well, she wouldn't have been good company anyway. After her meeting, Claire decided to have a walk around. Having dreamt about Mark all night, she thought it might exorcise his memory in some way.

Passing a mirror on her way down the stairs, Claire cast a look at her appearance. Her face looked pale and drawn, and to spite herself for wasting sleep over Mark, she hadn't bothered to make much of an effort to cover the effects of her sleepless night.

'What a mess!' she muttered, continuing on her way, and she wasn't just referring to her appearance. Her whole life seemed to be falling at her feet.

'Off home now?' George, one of the older security guards cast a smile at

Claire as they passed in the foyer.

'Yes, George. Goodnight!'

'Want me to see you out?' the man asked.

'No thanks!' she called opening the door. However, as she crossed the road to her car, she had an uneasy feeling and wished she had taken George up on his offer.

'Don't be so daft, woman!' she scolded herself as she started the engine. As music filled the car, she felt better than she had all day, and pulled out into the traffic.

Sitting in his own car, Mark looked at the piece of paper he held in his hand. On it was the phone number that Gemma had given him. He had stuck to his original intention of heading straight for Edinburgh, but having got as far as the Scottish border, he had turned back and had been sitting outside the nightclub for about an hour. He was consumed with thoughts about Claire, even though he had tried to forget her. Now, having seen her again, he was filled with thoughts of what might have been had they married, and had children.

He realised that the agitation he had felt earlier was not directed at Gemma, but at Claire. He wanted to make Claire tell him why she had left, what had gone so wrong that she couldn't talk to him about it. He had always believed that they were as close as any two people could be, that they shared everything. And when she had gone, his life was nothing.

Now he held in his hand a way of getting in touch with Claire, a way to finally exorcise a ghost from his past. He thought back to all the phone numbers he had been given by all the women he had come into contact with throughout his career with a smile. He had saved every single one in the beginning, in case his luck ran out. Not once had he ever phoned one of those women. Now, he was in possession of the one and only number he had ever wanted over the last seven years, and he couldn't bring himself to use it.

Resolutely screwing up the piece of paper and rolling down the window, Mark was just about to throw it away when he saw Claire walking across the street to a car. Mark watched silently, noticing the way the lamplight caught the auburn tones in her chestnut hair as she reached up to free it from its work-day ponytail. The well-cut jacket she wore emphasised her slim figure, and the short skirt showed her long, slim legs off to perfection as she strode quickly to her car.

As she pulled off, Mark pulled out behind her. He had to concentrate fully on his driving whilst trying to keep up with Claire. She was obviously used to the roads and the other drivers. He had always driven them around London when they had lived together. She had relied on him for a lot of things, and each new facet of her independence that he discovered, starting with her daughter, made him more determined to find out for himself just what kind of person Claire had become.

Finally, out of the city and on a dark country road, Mark could relax the tight grip he held on the steering wheel of the Range Rover. He was a fair distance behind Claire's dark blue family car, and hoped that she wasn't paying too much attention to what was behind her. Shortly, they came to another road and then Claire pulled into a driveway.

As Claire parked the car in the garage and closed the garage door, she experienced the same uneasy feeling she'd had earlier. Casting a quick glance at the road and seeing nothing, she smiled to herself at her jumpiness. She unlocked the front door and stepped gratefully out of the cold November air into the warm cottage.

Mark parked at the end of the driveway when he was sure that Claire was inside, and looked at her home. It was an old farmhouse, with white-washed walls and a thatched roof. With a wry smile, he remembered that this was exactly the type of house Claire had always talked about buying once they were married.

Mark watched lights come on as Claire moved from room to room, drawing the curtains. This cosy, domestic routine sent a feeling of emptiness through him. Lucky man, he thought, as he considered whoever it was Claire had chosen as a partner.

This man was Claire's husband, of that he had no doubt. She had been a firm believer that children should not be born out of wedlock. But still, Mark did not like to picture Claire sharing things with someone else that she had once shared solely with him. The more he thought about it, the sicker he felt. He needed to have it out with her, or else he would never be able to settle.

In one movement, Mark took the keys from the ignition and stepped out of the car. Without giving himself time to think, he strode up the driveway, and rang the doorbell.

Claire was coming down the stairs,

shrugging on an over-sized sweater, when she heard the doorbell. Wondering why Cari hadn't used her key, Claire opened the door with a smile on her face.

'Lost your key?' she asked brightly, and then she saw who her visitor was. The smile, along with every vestige of colour, faded from her face like the setting sun. Her heart began to hammer as she fought to catch her breath. She was standing face to face with a ghost from her past on her own front doorstep, and it was something that she had never planned for. Her home was the one place she didn't have to maintain her cold façade, where she didn't have to worry about anyone hurting her fragile heart. And now, Mark was here.

'I don't suppose you'd like to ask an old friend in for a cup of coffee? It's a bit nippy out here.'

'What are you doing here?' she said, her eyes blank. 'How did you get my address?'

Mark frowned. Claire seemed washed out to him somehow; diluted, as if all the spirit she once possessed had been broken. Little did he know that he had been the one to break it.

'That's not a question I usually get asked, Claire. Most people would be thrilled to have me turn up on their doorstep,' he joked.

Claire didn't hear the joke, only the narcissism, and it did not sit well with her. She remembered then why she disliked the effect fame had on people. All vestiges of normality and humility seemed to disappear. Gone, for sure, was the man she had known.

'Well, I'm not most people, Mark. I thought you would have taken the hint last night.'

'I assumed it was just a surprise to you. That's what Lee told me this afternoon.'

'You've spoken to Lee?' Panic rose in her. Oh God, she could feel the cloying sensation returning, stronger than ever. Everything was encroaching on her.

'I stopped by the club to see you, but you weren't there. I had a nice chat with him instead. And I met Cari and Gemma.'

'Gemma!' At the mention of her daughter's name from this man's lips, she suddenly felt faint.

'She, at least, was pleased to see me!' Mark smiled as if it amused him, but one look at Claire's face told him that the irony was lost on her. 'Claire?'

She felt anger coursing in her blood, filling every vein, until she thought she would explode. How the hell he could stand there, after what he had done to her, acting as if nothing had ever happened between them?

'Go, Mark. I don't want you here. I don't want anything to do with you.' Her voice was as cold as ice.

'I just want to talk about us.'

'There is no 'us'! There hasn't been for seven years, and that's the way I'd like to keep it,' she exclaimed, her voice trembling as she tried to control the seething anger inside her. 'I don't know what you want, Mark. But whatever it is, you can leave me out of it.'

Mark regrouped. Her icy tone had acted as a smack in the face and reminded him exactly why he was there. With this thought in mind, he answered, 'What I want, Claire, is a chance to talk about what happened. You left me, without any explanation. Don't you think I deserve at least that?'

'I don't think you deserve anything! Just leave, damn it!' His very presence, everything about him, was irritating her. And she certainly wasn't going to put up with it on her own doorstep.

'Let me in.'

'Which part of 'go away' don't you understand, Mark? I don't owe you anything, especially after the way you treated me. Now leave. Or do I have to call the police?' Claire's voice was low and held a warning, and her cheeks were suffused with red, both from her anger and from the chill wind blowing. She did not know how beautiful she looked with the light from the hallway shining behind her, making her auburn highlights glow.

'What do you mean, the way I treated you?'

Claire was just about to tell him, in no uncertain terms, when she saw the headlights of a car as it turned into her driveway. Panic bubbled in her throat when she recognised it as Lee's. She did not want Gemma to see Mark again.

'Mark, please. Leave, now,' she begged him, and the softening in her face intrigued him.

'Who is it?' he asked, turning as the car came to a stop.

'Mark!' Gemma's voice carried through the still night.

Mark heard Claire moan softly, and glanced at her briefly to see her face pale once more and her eyes close.

'Hey, Gemma! Hello, Lee; Cari,' Mark greeted them, with a smile.

Claire heard the crunch of the gravel beneath everyone's shoes. All three of them greeted Mark warmly, as though he were a seldom-seen member of the family. She smiled automatically as Lee shooed Cari, Gemma and Mark inside the house.

'How did the meeting go?' Lee asked, as Claire shut the front door.

'What?' Claire's mind was racing as she tried to process the situation she found herself in.

'The meeting with the brewery rep. You did go, didn't you?' Lee frowned, as he hung up his coat and those belonging to Cari and Gemma.

'Yes, I went. It was okay. He wants us to do some promotion for a new beer they have coming in the New Year.' Claire's monotone caused Cari to look concerned.

'Are you okay, love?' Cari asked softly, as Lee followed Gemma and Mark into the large, comfortable room.

Claire nodded vaguely, before she said, almost to herself. 'What's he doing here?'

Gemma's sensitive ears caught the last question, and with shining eyes, she turned to her mother and flung her arms around her.

'Thank you, Mummy!'

Claire closed her eyes as she hugged her daughter back tightly, hoping and praying that they would both come out of this with their hearts intact.

'What's this for?' she asked brightly, determined not to let anyone see how agitated she was by Mark's presence, and also to stop any probing questions. Even though Cari knew a brief version of her history with Mark, she did not want to dredge up any more memories than she had to.

'For Mark.'

Claire flashed Mark a look that dared him to contradict Gemma's belief in her mother's magnanimity.

Had Mark had been about to say something to the contrary, the sight of mother and daughter together struck him dumb. All he could think about was how beautiful they looked together, about how he might have had the chance to be a part of this, had Claire not left.

'I didn't know that you had already met this afternoon.' Claire was beginning to feel that all the forces of fate were ganging up against her to make her give up the one thing that she had kept to herself all these years.

'Mark says I can get tickets for his concert, Mum!' Gemma loosened herself from her mother's arms and went to sit beside Mark on the sofa.

Again, that same smile curled around Mark's mouth, and she felt venom rise in her throat. What the hell was he playing at? Was he determined to get back at her through her daughter? Common sense reiterated itself, and Claire firmly told herself she was being too forward in her thinking. Whatever Mark had intended when he had knocked at her door, she had no proof that it involved Gemma. It had wholly to do with her, Claire, and from the look in Mark's eyes, she knew that she was going to have to deal with it.

'That's nice. Who'd like some tea?'

She straightened up, and took count. 'You need to go and get ready for bed, young lady. I know it's Saturday tomorrow, but it is way past your bedtime.'

Gemma, polite to the last, especially in front of company, did not put on her usual show of disinterest in going to bed; she seemed almost eager.

'Can Mark see my bedroom?'

'I'm not sure he wants to see . . . '

'I'd love to!' Mark stood and took Gemma's outstretched hand.

With a sigh, she followed them and heard Gemma's excited chatter as she went down the hall to the kitchen. With much muttering and banging about, she made the tea. Shortly, Mark entered the kitchen behind Claire, making her jump.

'Damn it, do you have to sneak up on people like that?' she exclaimed, on edge. 'Where's Gemma?'

'She's getting changed. I thought it only decent that I left her to it.' Mark smiled.

'That's probably the only decent thing you've done in years!' Claire mumbled, and then Mark was standing right in front of her. She caught her breath as she looked into his dark grey eyes and smelt the subtle fragrance of his cologne, wishing that her body was not such a traitor. She imagined that he could hear the frantic tattoo her heart was beating, responding to an age-old rhythm caused by his close proximity.

'What is it with you making me out to be such a fiend?' His words were slow, as if he too was affected by Claire's closeness. He was fascinated by the play of emotion across her face.

Unable to reply, Claire felt as though she was on a roller coaster that was running out of control, straight toward a sheer drop into the unknown. Mark seemed to be coming closer and closer to her; she could see his lips part and she realised that he was about to kiss her.

A breath shuddered in Claire's throat. She knew that she should be remembering the pain he had caused her, how he had taken her trust and broken it into tiny pieces. She owed it to her hard-won independence. But she knew deep down that she could not fight it; she didn't want to get away. As much as she had tried to forget, she was still the same nineteen-year-old girl who had been desperately in love with this man; this man, with whom she had shared so much.

They stood in tense silence, Mark moving ever closer to Claire. She could feel the warmth of his shallow breaths on her lips, could feel the expectant tingle of the touch of his mouth on hers, could almost taste the sweetness of his kiss.

Claire closed her eyes in readiness for the inevitable and held her breath — until the kitchen door swung open, and in one second, the dream-like trance she was in vanished. She met Cari's questioning glance.

'Gemma's come to say goodnight to Mark,' Cari announced breezily, noting how Mark had taken a step back from Claire upon their entrance, how charged the atmosphere was in the room.

'Will you tuck me in, please?' Mark realised that this request came from Gemma, who was looking up at him with adoration in her eyes. A glance at Claire showed tears of frustration shining in hers, and Mark couldn't help but note the difference between the two of them. Gemma was eager for his company, willing to spend time with him, hanging on his every word, whereas Claire had been remote and cold from the first second of their renewed acquaintance.

'If it's okay with your mum. I wouldn't want to step on anyone's toes.'

Claire realised that she was helpless to do anything to control the situation, unable to bring herself to say no and cause Gemma pain. Gemma was her life, and her happiness came way ahead of Claire's own.

A nod was all she could bring herself

to give. Claire gave a tight-lipped smile as Gemma kissed her goodnight, and watched as she led Mark by the hand, her pride obvious for everyone to see.

As they left the kitchen, Claire turned to face the sink so that Cari would not see the tears that were threatening to tumble. She clung to the edge of the counter, feeling weak. Being near Mark had sapped the strength from her — strength that she would need to fight the battle she was sure would come.

Cari saw that Claire's slight shoulders were shaking, and she gently placed a hand on her. For the second time that night, she asked the same question. 'Are you okay?'

Claire shook her head, not trusting herself to speak. Cari remained behind her and eventually Claire raised her head and turned around.

'I don't want him here, Cari. She's going to fall in love with him and he'll hurt her.'

'She's a little girl who just met her hero. Let her enjoy it.'

'For how long, Cari? You don't understand. I don't want him to ruin her life, like he ruined mine!' the younger woman exclaimed, and began to pace the length of the room.

'I do understand. You're using Gemma as an excuse so that you don't have to deal with the past. I'm right, aren't I?' Cari raised her hand to silence Claire's denial. 'What is it you're so scared of, Claire?'

'I told you what he did to me, how much he hurt me.'

'Yes, you did. And if you are over him, I can't see what threat he could possibly be to you.' Cari was pushing at those locked doors, and Claire didn't know how long she could keep everything barricaded up; she felt so weak.

'He'll find out,' Claire's whisper was one of pure desperation, and tears began to fall from her sad eyes. Cari waited until Claire looked at her.

'What, sweetheart? What's so bad that you don't want him to know?' It hurt Cari to see Claire in so much pain, and wished she could help her, but she would have to wait until it came from Claire's own lips. 'What is it?'

Claire took a deep breath to stop her tears, but the pressure of keeping her secret for all those years finally broke down every door, and as the tears fell in earnest, the words came.

'Mark is Gemma's father.'

The room was silent except for the sound of Claire's sobs and the soft sounds of comfort coming from Cari as she held her.

'I'm sorry,' she sobbed to Cari, but the woman just held her tighter, wondering how Claire could have possibly dealt with all that pain, without once ever letting it show.

The kitchen door opened quietly; Mark stood there watching. He had heard someone crying as he reached the foot of the stairs and the temptation to see if it was Claire had been over-whelming.

At that moment, Claire raised her

head from Cari's shoulder, and froze. Her heart stopped for a second before it resumed hammering in her chest, and she hastily wiped away any tears that lingered on her cheeks. Had he heard her confession to Cari? He looked impassive to the scene, and she was struck by his indifference. Cari turned and saw Mark, and Lee, who had come to find out what was taking so long to make his cup of tea.

'Where's my tea, Claire? A man could die of thirst if he waited for you.' Lee took in the scene, and whether he read the situation correctly or not, Cari could have sainted her husband. 'Oh, that's it. You two women have been gossiping! Typical!' He placed a hand on Mark's shoulder. 'Come on, Mark. Why don't you and I go down to the pub and let these two get on with it?'

'Actually, I was about to make a move. I think I've had enough excitement for one night. Gemma's just about worn me out with questions.'

Both Lee and Cari smiled. 'Pressures

of being a pop star, eh?' Lee slapped Mark on the back.

'It's a tough job, but somebody has to do it!' Mark joked, but when Claire looked at him, she could only see self-congratulation and smugness in his eyes.

He hadn't spoken to her, but Claire knew that his next words were meant just for her.

'Well, thanks for a fun evening. I'll see you later.'

Claire felt a sense of relief as she silently saw all three of them to the front door, waving goodbye, no smile. Hugging herself, she returned to the kitchen in a dazed state and sat down at the table. Her thoughts came slowly, as if stuck in tar. It was too much of an effort to make sense of anything that had happened that evening; it hurt her head. She could not even begin to fathom how heavy her heart felt.

She lay her head in her arms on the kitchen table, and let her mind drift, slowly falling asleep, remembering

Mark's cold promise, 'I'll see you later.' And she didn't have any strength left to banish the thought from her mind.

3

Cari was worried about Claire, and had called her five times already that morning, leaving messages each time. Lee had told her to stop fussing, and Cari, in a rare moment of anger, snapped.

'Lee, have you heard anything I've said to you in the last hour? Claire was crying last night, real tears. Yes, she is a grown woman, and yes, if it were anyone else, I would agree that they would ask for help if it was needed. But I really don't think that she knows how to ask.'

Lee looked stunned for a second, then said, 'If it really is as serious as you think, then it's between the two of them. Let Claire and Mark work it out.'

Claire had woken at four o'clock that morning, with a sharp pain in her neck and a splitting headache from sleeping hunched over the kitchen table. She still felt as though her head was a tar pit; thick, black, sticky thoughts all squashed together. She wanted to clear her mind, to take stock of all that happened, but she could hardly stand, let alone sort out her life. She dragged herself upstairs and fell into bed, fully clothed, and found herself asleep, dreaming a dream that she hadn't had since she was pregnant with Gemma . . .

She was in a stark white hospital room, standing in the corner. There was a young girl in the hospital bed, silent and unmoving. There was a puppy and a rat in the opposite corner. They were barking and squeaking at each other.

Moving slowly to the bed, she looked at the young girl and recognised herself, pale and still. Claire opened her mouth, but nothing came out, no sound at all. The puppy and the rat were still making noises, but the sounds had formed into words.

'It'll ruin you, Mark. You can't stay

here, think of your career.' The voice belonged to Justin, Mark's manager, who had taken on the appearance of a wizened old rat, with a pointy nose, long whiskers and beady little eyes.

Claire looked at the puppy, adoring eyes turned to Justin the Rat, his tongue flopping to the side of his mouth as he listened attentively to Justin's words.

'You need to call off the wedding, Mark. No wedding.'

'No wedding,' Mark panted.

'No!' Claire screamed silently. The only person to hear her was the girl in the bed. She met Claire's gaze and gave the rictus grin of the dead.

'No!' Claire whispered, as the chill from the girl's gaze travelled around her body.

'No!' The word was ripped from Claire's mouth, as the bright light of the hospital room faded.

Claire sat up in bed, and her glance immediately flew to the corners of her bedroom. The weak November sunlight was pouring through the window, directly into her eyes. It took her a few seconds to adjust, to realise that she had been dreaming, but the sense of helplessness she'd been feeling before had returned with a vengeance.

Cursing herself for having slept so late, and trying to shake off the lingering effects of the disturbing dream, she went into the bathroom and took a shower. Feeling no better afterwards, she looked at her reflection in the mirror and did not like what she saw. Her skin was ashen, her dark blue eyes were almost black, to match the circles under her eyes. With a sniff, she wrapped her wet hair in a towel, and belatedly remembered Gemma.

'Pip! Gemma!' Claire went to her bedroom door and called aloud. Walking down the hallway, she knocked briefly at Gemma's door before entering.

The sight that met her eyes tore at her already aching heart. Gemma was asleep, surrounded by every single piece of Mark Crofts memorabilia that she possessed. Mark's latest album was playing softly on the stereo, and Gemma was hugging a magazine which had Mark on its cover.

'Oh, Pip!' Claire's words were barely above a whisper. The little girl had a smile on her face; she looked so happy. Claire had let her daughter do the one thing she had sworn she never would; Gemma had fallen in love with Mark, and it was too late for Claire to do anything about it. She plodded back to her bedroom, halfheartedly waving a hair dryer in the general direction of her head, before dressing in the clothes she had fallen asleep in last night.

Upon entering the kitchen, she saw the signs of devastation that only a child can create whilst making breakfast for herself. She set about clearing up, glad to have something to occupy her mind. As she put the dirty crockery in the sink, Claire felt a shiver run down her neck, like someone was behind her, and memories of the previous night came flooding back to her; the way she had felt as Mark had been about to kiss her.

'Damn, damn, damn!' she exclaimed loudly, angry now at Mark for turning her life upside down. She had a sinking feeling that this was only the beginning. Well, she hadn't wanted anything to do with him seven years ago, and she certainly didn't want anything to do with him now!

'Hello, Mum!'

Claire whipped round to see Gemma standing there, already dressed, with a huge smile on her pretty face, her eyes shining. Claire could see Mark in every feature.

'What's wrong?' Gemma asked. 'You look tired.'

'I didn't sleep too well, that's all. I'm fine,' Claire lied. 'What are you all dressed up for?' she asked, looking closely at Gemma. She had her shoes and coat on for some reason. 'Where are you going?'

'Shopping, remember?' Gemma chirped brightly. She pulled her mother to the hallway, and got her coat down from the rack on the wall.

Claire frowned again. She had promised Gemma at the beginning of the week that they would go shopping for some new clothes. Claire had never felt less like walking around Newcastle in the sub-zero temperatures with the throngs doing their Christmas shopping, but despite her bad mood, she could not bring herself to disappoint her little girl.

⋆　⋆　⋆

A few hours later, after her own shopping trip in town, Cari made it to Lou's Lounge. The place was empty, except for a lone figure at the far end of the bar. The manager of Lou's Lounge looked up expectantly from reading the paper, and smiled warmly to see her.

'Hello, Cari. I wasn't expecting you today.'

'Hi, Daniel. I was Christmas shopping and decided to pop in. Lee had some business at the club, so I thought I had better put in an appearance.' Cari smiled as Daniel relieved her of her load. 'Thanks, love. How's it been?'

'Not bad really, but it's early yet. We've had one or two in.' Daniel nodded his head at the man at the end of the bar. 'I expect it'll pick up later.'

Cari smiled as Daniel went to serve a new customer and glanced again at the other occupant of the bar. She thought she recognised him, and then he looked up as if he sensed her gaze.

'Mark!' Cari smiled in surprise, and he returned her smile. Cari took her coat off and took a seat on the stool next to him. One of his songs was playing.

'Did you put this on?' She nodded to the juke box behind her, and Mark grinned wryly. 'What are you doing here? Obviously not drinking!' She noted that his glass was nearly full. 'Is there something wrong?'

'What do you mean?' Mark looked at her warily.

'With my beer?'

'Oh!' He looked relieved, and shook his head. 'No, not at all. See!' He picked up the glass and took a swig. 'Lovely. I haven't tasted such good beer in a long time. This place is really nice. Feels comfortable.'

'Thank you!' Cari smiled. 'That was what we intended when we opened it. I'm proud of it.'

'And so you should be. It must be nice to go home at night and know you've made a success of something.'

'You make it sound as though you never have. Don't you feel like that too? What about all those number one records of yours?'

Mark looked at her and sighed. 'It's nothing physical though, Cari. I go home to an empty house. Yes, I've had hit records, and made lots of money, but it's not the same. It's nothing that I can actually see, or touch. I envy you that!' He picked up his drink.

Cari raised her eyebrows at his words. Here before her was the most popular entertainer in the world of pop music, dynamically good-looking to boot, and yet he looked for all the world like a man who had nothing. His muscular shoulders were slouched, there was day-old stubble on his chin, and a look in his eyes that told her he was tired. She did not know what to say, and instead repeated her earlier question.

'What are you doing here, anyway?'

'I've been rattling around the hotel all morning going crazy. I just felt like coming down to see what kind of place Claire worked in all those years. It's a lot different from the record store she used to manage.'

Cari smiled. 'She had a hell of a time when she first came.'

'Yeah?' Mark sat up straighter, interested. 'I'm sorry. Would you like a drink?'

'I'll have a gin and tonic, please.'

As Daniel poured her regular drink, Cari smiled her thanks.

'This is one drink that is practically

impossible to mess up, but Claire managed to do it.'

'I can imagine!' Mark smiled. 'She'd never worked behind a bar when I knew her. She much preferred to be in front of it with a pint in her hand.'

'Well, she definitely had beer on her hands the first night she started. A customer came in and ordered a gin and tonic, a pint of Guinness and a bloody Mary. I thought Claire was going to ruin me that night. She put lemonade in the gin and tonic, and left the beer glass under the pump and forgot it was running whilst she tried to figure out what exactly went into a bloody Mary. She flooded the bar, used about a tablespoon of Tabasco, and lost me a few regulars!'

Mark joined Cari in her laughter.

'To her credit though, she always remained calm; never got flustered if a customer gave her a hard time,' Cari added. 'By the end of the first week, I knew I had a hard worker, and look where she is now! Publicity manager at the biggest club in the North.'

'She's done well,' Mark mused. 'She has a lovely home. How long has she lived there?'

'About four years. It was in a right state when they moved in, but she quickly knocked it into shape.'

'They?' Mark questioned, and then remembered. 'Oh yes. What does he do?'

'Who?' Cari looked puzzled.

'Claire's husband.' Mark looked at Cari, wondering why she was frowning.

'Claire's not married.'

Mark raised an eyebrow. 'Boyfriend?'

'Nope. She's never shown any interest in men as long as I've known her. Not that she hasn't had any offers. She's a beautiful girl.'

Mark was not listening to Cari as he processed this new information. No husband, no boyfriend, and yet Claire had a daughter. This was confusing him. Claire had always been so adamant about only having children once she was married? How had she changed so much from the way she was?

'Then what about Gemma's father? Where's he?' Mark looked Cari in the eye, and for a second, the woman panicked. She was not comfortable with the turn the conversation had taken.

Cari shrugged, and picked up her drink. 'Claire's never mentioned it.' *Before now*, a little voice whispered. 'She turned up here, and then five months later, along came Gemma. We've never asked her. It didn't seem to matter.'

'When did she get here, Cari?' He was wondering what kind of person Claire had become. A child out of wedlock, a single mother, the father of her child gone. This was not the person he remembered. He wanted to know many things, and, if Claire was unwilling to face him, he would have to find out another way.

'Almost exactly seven years ago. We were hiring extra staff for Christmas.' Cari could see Mark was deep in thought, and sensed the powerful emotions he was feeling, so she remained quiet. She wondered momentarily if she had made a mistake in giving him that information. What would he do with it? Would he make the connection?

As she was thinking, Mark stood abruptly. She looked at him in surprise.

'Going already?' she asked.

'Yes. Thanks for the chat, Cari. I'll see you again soon.' Mark took his jacket off the back of the stool and shrugged it on. Cari noted that the black leather coat was very expensive; now he looked more like the superstar he was. The tired look was gone from his eyes, but their grey colour had darkened and there seemed to be a tightness in the set of his jaw. He was a very determined man, whatever he was about to do.

'I hope so,' she replied, and watched him leave.

At that moment, Claire was trying hard not to lose her temper with her daughter. Gemma had played merry hell with her mother's nerves all afternoon, and Claire was wishing that she had never made the promise.

'That's it, Pip! I've had enough,' Claire exclaimed as Gemma tugged her into yet another shop. Gemma pouted.

'But Mum..!' Her whine turned the word into almost three syllables and Claire finally lost it. She pulled Gemma into the shop doorway and bent down to look at her.

'I said enough. I really don't enjoy traipsing around town on a Saturday, and I enjoy listening to your moaning even less. I've still got food shopping to do yet, so button it, okay?'

The little girl had rarely seen her mother in such a bad mood; it was even rarer that she raised her voice to her.

Claire insisted that Gemma sit in the little seat in the shopping trolley, despite the fact that she was far too big for it, telling her that she wanted to get around the supermarket as quickly as possible. Gemma was very uncomfortable, and spent the whole thirty minutes banging her feet against the metal caging, the tinny noise grating on Claire's already frayed nerves.

By the time they got to the checkout, after being fifth in the queue, Claire's patience with Gemma, and absolutely everything else, had worn thin. When she saw the cashier's name tag declaring he was a trainee, her sigh of impatience could not have been any clearer. Claire's cold, irritated stare throughout the whole check out procedure made the clerk so nervous, he made more and more mistakes, until finally, Claire sarcastically offered to get behind the counter and do it herself.

Gemma watched the scene quietly. It was only when her mother had finished loading the car with groceries, and they were both inside that the little girl spoke.

'You was rude to that man, Mummy.' Her indignant voice filled the silence in the car in between Claire doing up her seat belt and putting the key in the ignition. 'You told me not to be rude.'

'And?' Claire looked at her daughter briefly before starting the engine. It did not catch the first time, and successive tries were not fruitful. Claire began to swear under her breath.

Gemma was holding her breath, trying not to cry. This was the first time in her life that she had never experienced 'do as I say, not as I do'. She was confused as well as upset, not realising that her mother had been angry before they even left the house; she thought that she was to blame.

'Bloody car!' Claire shouted as she tried the ignition one more time. 'Bloody stupid car!'

But part of being a single parent was coping, and she had taught herself just enough to cover the basics of car maintenance. She checked the water in the radiator reservoir, tried to see if the oil level was alright — but it was too dark to tell — and finally wriggled some wires in the region of the battery, then slammed the bonnet shut.

Getting back in the car, she was shivering from the frigid air outside. She turned the engine over and it started first time. Gemma looked at Claire warily, then flashed her a grin.

'Well done, Mum!' The little girl was relieved to see the frown was gone from Claire's face.

'Thanks. Now, let's go home.'

Both Claire and Gemma were quiet on the drive home. Gemma was thinking about Mark and all the new clothes she had been bought, and her eyelids were drooping with the warmth from the heater. Claire was also thinking about Mark, but along entirely different lines.

She had lost control of the situation with Mark and Gemma, and now she was losing control of herself, of her emotions, and it was down to him. She had almost turned to putty in his hands with his closeness yesterday. He was so damned sure of himself, so secure, that she felt weak and pitiful next to him.

Claire knew that she was not like that anymore. She used to cling to Mark because she had no one else. Now, it was different. She had Gemma, she had friends, she had her pride. There was no way she was going to let him get to her. She was strong, she knew what she wanted for herself and her daughter, and Mark did not figure in those plans at all.

So how come she was falling to pieces inside? He was only as much to her as she let him be, but there was still part of her that responded to the past they had shared. Was that why she had been almost ready to accept his kiss last night? Was she that lonely? No, she told herself firmly. She had Gemma now, she had all she needed. But she couldn't deny that Mark had awakened good memories of the physical closeness they had enjoyed.

Her thoughts drifted to the remembrance of Mark's body pressing against hers. It was as if the car was on automatic pilot, because Claire found herself bringing the car to a halt in the driveway without having been conscious of the journey home. Unconscious too, of the Range Rover that was parked out on the road.

'We're home, Pip.' Claire reached over and shook the sleeping Gemma gently. She woke up, stretching and yawning. Sleepily, she looked at her mother 'Let's get inside quickly. It's too cold to stay out here.'

Claire opened the boot and handed Gemma her goodies. She leaned back into the car to grab the majority of the grocery bags, and as she straightened up she saw Mark on her doorstep, and Gemma running towards him, bags flying.

'Mum, Mark's come for dinner.'

Claire looked at Mark's face but couldn't read his expression, as his face was in the shadows.

'Has he, now?' she asked, as she walked past the two of them to the front door.

'*I'm* glad you're here!' Gemma said, quietly.

'Doesn't look like your mum's very pleased about it!' Mark said, coming to rescue the bags from Claire as she tried to balance them on one hip whilst trying to get the key in the door. Mark's hand brushed hers, and she glanced at him nervously.

'I can manage,' she muttered, and was sure she could feel Mark smiling at her ineptitude. Opening the door, she entered and heard Gemma's stage whisper to Mark as they followed her in.

'She's in a bad mood.' And with that, Gemma reeled off all the separate incidents as if they were crimes against humanity, ending with the supermarket cashier. Mark laughed aloud at that one.

Claire had been putting the groceries away, but when she heard his laughter she peeked around an open cupboard door and was momentarily transfixed by what she saw. Gone was any arrogance from his stance as he leaned against the table, his grey eyes sparkling; Claire could see the image of the man she once knew. Their gaze collided, and the smile faded from his face. His eyes searched hers for a long moment before she tore hers away, unsettled. She had been angry at him all day, because he was rude, arrogant and thought himself to be superior, and now, she had seen him as he had been when she last knew him, and her heart did not know what to believe.

'Mum, I want to show Mark my clothes,' Gemma announced, making Claire jump.

'Hang on, Gemma. Before you start your fashion show, we'd better check with your mum to see if I can actually stay to dinner.' Mark turned a questioning glance to Claire, and she looked from him to Gemma, whose eyes were shining brightly. Two pairs of clear grey eyes were on her, and Claire realised for the first time exactly how alike the two of them looked.

'We're not having anything exciting. I hadn't planned on company.' Claire looked helplessly at her daughter. If only Gemma had been older, not so devoted to her idol, then Claire might have been able to put a stop to this before it started. But she knew that was not going to happen now. Unwittingly, the six-year-old had opened old wounds in Claire's heart, and her only hope was that Gemma would not end up the same way, wishing she had never met Mark Crofts, never fallen in love with him, and never let herself be hurt.

'That's fine with me.' Mark's voice sounded strangely quiet to Claire. She could hear warning bells ringing in her head, but as yet, could not find a single clue, no obvious evidence from Mark as to what his intentions were.

Gemma was eager to show off her new clothes, so Claire banished them both from the kitchen, shooing them out like a mother hen, whilst she finished putting the shopping away and set about preparing some kind of meal.

Mark looked back at her just as she shut the door, and she turned away because she did not want him to see how unsure she was about her feelings for him.

Mark settled himself in the cosy living room whilst Gemma paraded up and down in her new clothes. In between outfit changes, Mark had time to think back over his conversation with Cari earlier in the day. When he had discovered that Gemma's father was not around, and put it together with the information that Claire had been pregnant upon her arrival in Newcastle, something had shifted inside him, and had left him feeling very uneasy.

'She's not married. She turned up here, and then five months later, along came Gemma.'

There was something missing from the story of Claire's life since she had left London, and he knew that when he found it, he would know exactly what was making him so crazy. It was the same thing that had led him to Claire's house, that urged him to wait in the cold on her doorstep until she returned. He knew he wanted to confront her about her desertion, but there was more to it than that. She might have changed, but not so completely that Mark could not tell that she was frightened of something, hiding something. He had seen it in her eyes.

Her eyes. Those same eyes that had been haunting his dreams of late. He had seen darkness in her eyes, each time she looked at him. He could see other things too, different emotions from the ones he remembered. Gemma had finished her show by then; her own shining eyes and bright smile had made him happy. He wondered if all little girls loved showing off like that, and it bothered him that he had no experience with children to answer his question. Lots of things bothered him; what he had seen last night, Claire crying.

Claire had been thinking much along the same lines and had come to the conclusion that she had been angry with herself for letting Mark see her vulnerability. She had been so strong over the years, bringing Gemma up on her own. She knew how to deal with unwanted attention from admiring men, but Mark had unsettled her in a matter of minutes. She needed to be stronger than that, to stop him from having an effect on her. But as Mark entered the kitchen and she met his long look, her heart skipped a beat and she knew it was going to be an uphill battle.

'Has she finished her fashion show?' Claire kept her tone even, not wanting to give Mark any chance to latch on to her sense of helplessness in his presence.

'Yes. She's upstairs changing now. I don't remember you liking clothes that much.'

'I don't!' Claire looked across the table at him as she set the places.

'She must get it from her father, then.' It was an innocent comment, but one that sent ice through Claire's veins.

'Where is he, anyway?'

Claire dropped the cutlery on the table. She had not expected such a direct question. What was he doing? As far as she knew, his only interest was in her, not Gemma. Her heart was pounding in her chest, and in her ears, as the blood tumbled around her body.

'He's not around,' she mumbled and carried on with her task.

Mark frowned momentarily, and wondered where to go from here. He felt the sense of confusion return, and wished he knew what it was he was after. Something was making him ask these questions, but he did not know why. There was something he needed, but what was it?

'I haven't seen any pictures of him around.'

Look in the mirror, Claire's inner voice screamed at him. 'There aren't any.'

'Why not?'

'What's this got to do with you? I thought you came here to hassle me, not Gemma.' Claire turned to him, angered now by his questions. She had no idea why he wanted to know, but it made her extremely uncomfortable and she did not want to feel that way in her own home.

'I'm not hassling you, Claire. I haven't mentioned anything about you and me, have I?'

'Then say what you have to and be done with it. I told you that I don't want you around, Mark. The only reason you're here at all is because of my daughter. For some reason, she adores you, and I don't want to hurt her.'

'What about hurting me?'

'What?' Claire gave him an incredulous look. He was making it sound as if he had been a victim in all of this, and needed the compassion and support of everyone. 'Hurting you?'

'Yes.'

'Bull. It's your pride that's been hurt. How could anyone possible leave Mark Crofts, the superstar?' Her sarcastic tone was not lost on him.

'That's not what I meant. For whatever reason, you're making me out to be the bad guy, and I think I have a right to know why.' He resumed his look of hurt, and Claire could see in his stance exactly how much he measured his worth. He fully expected her to tell him everything, as if it was his God-given right.

'You really don't know, do you?'

'Know what? If I knew, do you think I'd be here? Don't you think I have better things to do?' His petulance showed on his face.

'You were the one who came here, uninvited, I might add! Does it make you feel good, knowing that you've made a child's day just by your very presence? I'm just glad I got out when I did. There's no way on this earth that I could have stayed with you. Look at you. You honestly think you're better than me, don't you, because you have more money, and the adulation of millions. I hope that keeps you happy,

Mark, because you have nothing else. One day, when it's all over, you'll look back and know that you messed up when it came to you and me. I know you think it was all my fault, and you can think that. I really don't give a damn. I don't even care anymore. There was always someone or something else between us, but you couldn't see that. I really don't want to have anything to do with you.'

Claire had hardly taken a breath, and her chest was heaving with the force of the emotions behind her words. Mark was looking at her, not knowing what to make of it. He had only taken in bits of what she had said as it had come tumbling from her mouth.

'I don't understand you. I don't understand why you left, and I certainly don't understand why you had Gemma outside of marriage.'

Claire stared at him, open-mouthed. Where in the hell had that come from? They had not been talking about that, and she could see from the expression on his face that the words had slipped out unconsciously.

'I . . . I don't see what that's got to do with anything,' Claire stammered, stopping dead in her tracks. She had been ready to deal with his questions on her leaving him, but this had come out of the blue. It was a full-on attack, it went straight to the centre of her, and she wondered again if Mark had overheard her conversation with Cari the night before.

Mark's mind was racing towards something, but he didn't know what. He was relying on his gut instinct. He could see for himself that all the wind had gone out of Claire's sails following her gutsy speech, and she now seemed to be drifting, clinging tightly to something which she was terrified to let go of.

'I want to know how you managed to turn up in Newcastle, pregnant, just a few weeks after you left me. And how you had Gemma only five months later.'

Claire sank onto a chair and tried to calm her thoughts. As she sat down, she felt as if Mark was towering way above her. He was getting to her, but any anger that she might have had was replaced by an urgent sense of fear. Mark was getting closer to her secret.

A thought struck her then as funny, and she sort of smiled. She could manage to plan publicity operations and Lee's business like clockwork, but when it came to the machinations of her own life, and her heart, she was clueless. Mark saw her slight smile, and thought instantly of her words: 'There was always someone or something else between us, but you couldn't see that.'

Always someone else. Anger coursed through him, as he made the connection that he thought he had been searching for all afternoon.

'You were sleeping with someone else. How could you do that to me? I loved you!' Mark leaned across the table, until he was just inches from her face, and Claire drew some strength from his unjustified anger.

'Don't you dare! Like you never had anything else in your life. What about Justin, the band, your bloody career!' She came halfway out of her seat until their faces were almost touching. She could see the stubble on his chin, the jet flecks in his eyes, and the dark circles beneath. She wanted to yell and scream at him, but the remaining spirit left her. She sank back into the chair, and put her head in her hands.

'I never slept with anyone else, Mark. There's never been anyone else.' Her voice was barely above a whisper, yet the honesty he heard there rang loud and as clear as a bell.

'Then . . . ' He looked into her tired eyes, and saw tears. His mind was reeling with a discovery, and he did not know what to do or how to feel.

A hissing sound filled the room, and Claire registered that the pan on the stove behind her was boiling over. Every part of her ached as she hauled herself out of the chair. Now he knew, and she felt as if she had sold the last piece of her soul to the devil. She had surrendered all control to Mark now.

Mark was still standing, watching Claire, but not seeing her. His focus was inwards, dealing with what he had heard. He did not know where to start to clear his foggy mind, but at that moment, the door opened and in came Gemma.

'I'm hungry,' she chirped, taking her seat at the table.

Claire turned from her task slowly, and saw Gemma. She looked at Mark then, and watched as his gaze lifted to Gemma — his daughter.

4

Gemma seemed completely unaware of the dour faces of the two adults as she laughed and joked her way through the meal of spaghetti that her mother had served up. As far as she was concerned, everyone was as happy as she herself was. She was eating her favourite food, with her favourite rock star, and had lots of new clothes to boot. Gemma was having a great time.

But as for Claire and Mark . . . The look of utter shock on his face when he had made the final connection just a few minutes earlier had told Claire that Mark really hadn't had a clue. Watching him now, she was sure that he was having a hard time dealing with it. His gaze had met Claire's just once since, and there was nothing there that could have given her a clue as to what he was feeling. Her heart contracted at the thought of his confusion and then she gave herself a mental kick.

What did she care how he felt? She hadn't wanted to tell him about it, hadn't wanted him to know, but he had to keep pushing; as stubborn and as arrogant as he was, he felt like he had a right to know about Claire's life since she'd left him. Well, now he did, and he was going to have to deal with it in his own way. The only thing that Claire had to worry about was Gemma. She wasn't going to let her be hurt.

Dinner finished after what seemed an eternity in an interminably long day. Even Gemma looked tired by this point.

'How about an early night for once, Pip?' Claire asked, as Gemma came to lollop against her, resting her head on her shoulder.

'Can Mark read to me?'

Claire looked at him washing the dishes, and he raised an eyebrow in question. There seemed to be so much that small movement asked, but she simply nodded.

'Yes, sweetheart. Go on up and get ready for bed.'

''Night, Mum!' Gemma kissed her mum resoundingly on the cheek and then looked expectantly at Mark. Claire watched as a slight frown creased the little girl's brow, and turning, she looked questioningly at Mark.

He was still busy washing up, acting as if he was not aware of Gemma's presence. Claire felt a surge of anger rush through her, sure that he was now trying to figure out a way to get out of the situation, and she was not going to let him upset Gemma.

'Mark!' Her tone was sharp, and he turned his head quickly, his eyebrows raised in question.

'Oh! Hey!' He smiled at Gemma, as he turned and dried his hands on a towel. The creases disappeared from Gemma's brow, and she returned his smile. 'I was miles away!'

Or wishing you were, Claire thought,

acidly. 'Thank you for washing up,' she said out loud.

Mark shrugged. 'You might have to do it again. It's been a long time since I actually washed up anything.'

'Well, we can't all have a maid do all the housework!'

Gemma did not notice the caustic tone of her mother's voice and looked intrigued.

'You have a maid?' She looked up at Mark.

'I'm afraid so!'

'So do you, Gemma. Me. Now, off to bed. Mark can't be hanging around here all night.' Far from being considerate to Mark, she wanted to let him know he wasn't welcome to stay any longer than was necessary.

Claire sat in an armchair in the living room, and tried to make herself relax. Usually, she enjoyed the silence and the stillness at this time of night, after a long day at work and the hectic hours with Gemma before she went to bed. But tonight, she could not bear to sit still, could not stand the silence, when she knew that Mark was upstairs, maybe working on her daughter, making her fall even more in love with him, plotting to take her away where Claire could have nothing to do with her.

That thought scared Claire into movement. Not once before had she considered the possibility that Mark may want Gemma for himself. Climbing the stairs two at a time, she tried to tell herself that she was being silly, but the thought had planted a seed of mistrust in her mind, and it was growing rapidly. Hearing no sound coming from Gemma's bedroom, Claire opened the door, very quietly and very slowly, hoping not to disturb them. Gemma's bed was on the wall opposite the door, and luckily, Mark was seated at the edge of it, with his back turned, blocking any view of the doorway. Claire watched with her breath held through the crack in the door as Mark leaned in to kiss

Gemma good night. Claire knew from her daughter's voice that she was almost asleep.

''Night 'night, Mark.'

'Goodnight, Gemma.'

Mark moved as if to straighten up, when Claire heard Gemma's voice again.

'I wish you was my daddy.'

With a barely stifled sob, Claire pulled the door to, and covered her mouth with her hand as she leaned against the wall, taking deep breaths, trying to stop herself from crying. Gemma's softly spoken words had torn a hole wide in Claire's heart. She knew that Gemma's six-year-old mind did not fully comprehend why she should be so different from all her friends. Even the ones whose parents were divorced had some kind of contact with their fathers, whereas Gemma had none.

Claire had told Gemma a long time ago that just because she only had a mummy, it didn't mean that she wasn't normal, just that her mummy loved her twice as much, and Claire had honestly believed that it was enough. But Gemma was now at an age when comments made by her peers were beginning to hurt.

Claire walked to her own bedroom, and entered the bathroom. There she rinsed her face in cold water, and spoke harshly to her reflection in the mirror. She needed to have the strength to deal with this in a way that would not hurt Gemma.

Checking herself in the mirror, her outward appearance one of normality even if her insides were still churning at the prospect of having to face Mark, Claire once more went to check on Gemma, only to find that Mark was still there as she opened the door. He was sat on the chair by the end of the bed, staring at the sleeping figure. Claire couldn't help but remember the time she had been in hospital, when he spent time in a chair looking at her, too. She also remembered the dream she'd had the night before, and hardened her heart. Mark turned his gaze to the doorway, and saw Claire watching him with a cold expression. They looked at each other for a moment, and then he rose.

Claire stood back to let him pass and then closed the door behind him. He had not moved much further than a foot, and she found herself rather closer to him than she would have liked. She moved away from him, hoping that he would follow her downstairs, not wanting to have any confrontation where Gemma may awaken and hear. The creak of the stairs behind her told her that he had followed her lead, and she wondered whether she should take him into the living room or the kitchen, where at least she could put the large table between them.

'Tea or coffee?'

Mark pulled out a chair and sat down heavily. 'I don't suppose you have anything stronger?'

'Well, I've got some beer, or wine. I

don't keep any spirits in the house, what with Gemma and everything.'

'Whatever you're having.'

Mark looked tired, older somehow, and he was quiet for a long time, twisting the wine glass by the stem, watching the pink liquid dance near the rim, without spilling over. As Claire watched him, she dared the wine to spill over onto the table, not so much for the fact that she would then have something to do, other than watch him and wait for him to speak, but more so that she could feel that he did not have total control: control over the liquid in the glass, control over the way the conversation would go, control over her whole future. She had drained her own glass by the time he had even taken a sip from his, and as she stood to refill it, she found his gaze on her.

'Were you ever going to tell me?' His question seemed to fill the entire room, it was so silent, and Claire felt it echoing in her head.

'Tell you what?'

'That Gemma is my daughter. She is, isn't she?' Mark's eyes narrowed, watching her closely, and she realised that this was probably her last chance to get out of this with her heart in one piece.

All she had to say was, 'No, Mark, she isn't yours. She's the product of a one-night stand.' But she couldn't bring herself to. She was too worried about Gemma getting hurt to attack anyone else. She could only defend what she had.

'Yes.'

Just one word. One word that said it all as far as Mark was concerned. The reason she had left him. It riled him no end, but their breakdown in relations was not the issue here. The fact that he had a daughter was. He looked at Claire with ice in his eyes, and she flinched, seeing the grey of his eyes turn almost black.

'Why?'

'Why what, Mark? Why didn't I tell you I was pregnant?'

'Yes! Claire, I have a daughter. How do you think that makes me feel? My child has been walking this earth for the past six years and I didn't know!'

Claire watched, entranced, and found herself enjoying his discomfort with the situation. She knew it was getting to him, and she was pleased. His frustration and annoyance were nothing compared to his betrayal of her; to the long nights she'd had to deal with Gemma as a baby, when she had fevers, colic, and the other hundreds of things that ail newborns. She looked at him and found that everything about him irritated her; his tan, his carefully cut hair, his expensive watch which was reflecting light onto the wine glass he was holding.

'I imagine it's a bit of a surprise.'

'Surprise,' he thundered, pushing back his chair and leaning across the table towards her. 'Stop playing games with me, Claire. You won't win!'

The threat in his voice was unmistakable, and a chill ran through Claire briefly, knowing that he meant business. But she too meant business and she had too much to lose not to fight him.

'I'm not playing games.' Her voice was low. 'Yes, you're Gemma's father, but that's just a biological fact I can do nothing about, as far as I'm concerned.'

'That's not fair. I didn't know anything about it. You just left.'

'Well, life's not fair, Mark. And don't act as if you're the one who's the injured party in all of this. It's not as if I disappeared off the face of the earth.'

'I looked for you!'

'What, personally, or did you have one of your 'maids' do it?' Claire's sarcasm was not lost on him.

Mark glanced at her and saw a slight smile on her lips. It looked almost as if she was enjoying this.

'I hired three different detectives to look for you. They scoured the whole country and came up with nothing!' There was honesty in his voice, but the whole thing just struck Claire as immensely funny.

Private detectives looking for her! How tacky could you get? She began to laugh, and annoyance flashed across his face as he continued.

'Of course, they were looking for Claire Mitchell, not Claire Montague. And they certainly weren't looking for someone with a baby.'

Claire was still laughing, but some hysteria was sneaking into the sound, her laughter ringing tinny and false. Mark stared at her, and she began to sober up, not because of the anger in his look, but because something he had said was just beginning to sink in. He had been hurt and worried enough about her to have someone try and find her. Claire blinked and looked at him anew. Had he really been that much in love with her, that he wanted to find her? His cold, hard stare made her doubt it, and she reminded herself of what had been discussed between him and Justin in her hospital room — and of what had led to her being in that hospital room in the first place.

'So now you've found me, and now you have a daughter. What are you going to do about it, Mark?'

'What do you expect me to do? It's shocked the hell out of me. To be all on my own one minute and then to find out I have a child; it's not an easy step to make.'

'Then don't make it. I didn't want you to know. Why do you think I didn't tell you?' She paused, then asked quietly, 'What do you want from me?'

'I don't know. I haven't thought that far. All I know is that I enjoy being with Gemma. Perhaps I can spend some time with her?'

'For how long?'

'What?' Mark put the glass down on the table. 'What do you mean for how long?'

'How long are you going to be around? Okay, so you have some free time now, but you have your career to think of.'

'There are ways.'

'No! I am not going to have

Gemma's hopes built up. I don't want her to have fleeting visits a couple of times a year. She deserves better than that.' And so do I, she thought silently, not wanting to have to cope with another broken heart.

'So what do you want? Do you want me to give up performing so that I can be a full-time father to her?' Mark's tone was biting, and Claire knew then that his career would once again come between them.

'I don't want anything from you. As far as I'm concerned you can go now, and forget all about us. We've managed fine without you around so far. Gemma doesn't know about you, she doesn't know that I even knew you before.'

'She doesn't know about us?' Mark's face softened and Claire felt a peculiar shiver run down her spine.

'What's to know? It's nothing to do with her. She doesn't need to know that her mother made mistakes when she was very young.'

'You think she's a mistake?'

'That's not what I said, Mark. Don't twist my words. Just go, please.'

'No, I won't. We're not finished. I want you to tell Gemma about me. I think she'd be quite pleased to have me as her father. She told me earlier that she wished I was . . . '

'I heard what she told you!' Claire snapped, hearing again the wistful tone of her daughter's sleepy voice. 'She doesn't know any better. She's just a little girl with a crush on Mark Crofts the rock star. She doesn't know you the way I do.'

'Was it that bad?' Mark looked at her with memories of nights of passion in his eyes, but Claire did not want to remember the good times. All she had brought with her from the relationship was Gemma and a broken heart.

'Forget it. I'm not telling her.'

'Then I'll tell her.'

'You think she'd believe you over her own mother? I'm the one who has looked after her these last six years, not you.'

'And whose fault is that? Not mine, Claire. If I'd known back then, I could have taken care of her, of you both.'

'How? With money, expensive gifts? It takes more than that to be a father, Mark. It takes things like commitment and time, neither of which you have to spare. Everything you do is for your career. It would have been like that, even if I had stayed with you.'

'How do you know?' Mark spat, angered at Claire's stubbornness.

'Because I can see it. Do you think you'd have been as popular with your fans if you were saddled with a wife and baby all those years ago? Do you think you would have found time away from your bloody career to spend time with Gemma? I don't think so.'

'I want you to tell her.'

'I won't.'

Mark stared at her. Claire was adamant. He knew that he could stand there and argue with her until he was blue in the face, but she wouldn't change her mind. He thought for a moment, all the while looking at her, frustration written all over his face. He was not entirely sure how he felt about having a daughter, but he wasn't going to allow Claire to deny his presence any longer. He would have to make her change her mind, force her even.

'Either you tell Gemma that I'm her father, or . . . ' He paused, and anger rushed through Claire's veins. How dare he make this into a performance? Why the hell was he trying to be so dramatic when she was his only audience?

'Or what?' She took his bait, snapping it around her tongue.

'Or I'll go to the press.'

Claire felt as if the bottom of her world had just fallen from beneath her, with her heart following suit. She could only stare at him, fear in her eyes.

Mark watched as the colour drained from her face. For a moment it looked as if she was going to pass out. With concern, he moved towards her as if to comfort her, but she stood and backed away with such speed that she stumbled and caught hold of the counter behind her for support.

How could he even suggest it? Did he not have any clue what it could do to Gemma? She was only a little girl, but he was prepared to turn her life into a media circus. Did he love media attention that much that he could not see the harm it did to people's private lives? Anything that had happened between Claire's own mother and father had made front page news, and Claire had had to deal with that at school. At first, all her friends had thought it was really cool, but then, when Claire refused to talk about it, they became mean, and teased her, calling her a show-off and a big-head. But she had been five years older than Gemma was now when it had started. A six-year-old had none of the defences needed to deal with that kind of attack, and Claire knew that children could be very unkind.

She turned tortured eyes to Mark, to

see if she could find any compassion in him, but all she came across was a brick wall. After what seemed an eternal silence, Claire spoke, her voice quiet, and full of pain.

'All right, I'll tell her.'

'Good!' Mark's smile refuelled her anger.

'You have to promise me that you won't tell anyone, especially the press,' she barked, her voice cracking.

'I won't. But I warn you, Claire, if you don't tell her, I will do something about it.' He paused briefly, as though he was giving her time for it to sink in. 'I'll call you tomorrow to make sure you have told her. And I'm going to check with my lawyer first thing on Monday to see where I can go from here.'

'Can't you give me until Monday? It will take her some time to get used to the idea. I don't want her upset.'

'I don't really think she'll be upset that I'm her dad!' Mark's tone was light, and Claire could see conceit in his eyes, but she did not want to fight with him anymore. All she wanted to do was sleep.

'Would you mind leaving now?'

'Sure.' He sounded deflated.

Opening the door for him, Claire hugged herself against the cold.

'I'm glad we got this sorted out, Mitch!'

His use of her old nickname cut her to the quick, and her response was snorted at him.

'Yeah, let's do it again soon!'

He frowned, and reiterated his warning. 'I meant it.'

'I heard you loud and clear the first time,' Claire barked, and stepping inside, she slammed the door in his face.

In the kitchen, Claire proceeded to drink her way through the rest of the bottle of wine until her angry thoughts began to dissipate; her mind was a jumble of pain and memory. In something of a daze, she made her way up to bed, and fell straight asleep, aided by the wine and the fact that she was both physically and mentally exhausted.

She awoke a few hours later though, to the sound of thunder crashing outside, and rain beating against the bedroom window. She was drenched with sweat and her heart was hammering, having had a nightmare about her father's funeral, something that she had not remembered for a long time.

Luke Mitchell had been her rock in life. When Claire's mother had embarked on her writing career and became a household name, Luke had been the one who had always been there for Claire. But then he had died in a fatal car crash and he was gone.

Claire's mother, Katie, had been asked to attend an awards ceremony given in her honour by one of the Literary Guilds in London, and Luke had accompanied her. Sweeping the floor at the awards, Katie had been in a jubilant mood, wanting to stay and celebrate with her fans, but Luke was tired after a long day at work and had wanted to get home. So they left, only to be pursued by the press, who wanted pictures of their darling. Luke took a short cut down a little-used country lane, which would bring them out to the other side of the village. From there, they could slip into their house unnoticed. But there had been a storm earlier that evening, that had brought down an old tree. By the time the headlights had cut through the gloom enough for him to see it and swerve, it was too late. The car hit the tree, and Luke was killed instantly. Katie miraculously escaped with a few cuts and bruises.

Claire's world had collapsed. Her father was gone, her mother was too caught up in her own grief to offer any comfort to her youngest daughter, and she'd had to cope with seeing the scene of the accident, the twisted wreckage of the car, plastered over every front page in the country. Since then, she had never read another newspaper, and had shut herself off from her family and the rest of the world.

As a bolt of lightning cracked outside, Claire flinched at the bright light. She was trembling from head to foot, and was surprised to taste salty tears on her lips. An empty feeling had settled over her, and it was not just due to remembering the loss of her father. It was a culmination of the demise of her relationship with Mark, and the threat of losing Gemma to Mark if she did not heed his warning.

Claire got up and went downstairs, reluctant to attempt sleep again for fear of another nightmare. The memory of her father's death was still with her, thanks to her mind's tortured tricks. She made herself a cup of tea, and settled in front of the television to try and banish her thoughts.

She awoke at dawn, having dozed off, suffering with a mighty headache. She never normally drank that much, but she found herself relieved to have another kind of pain to dwell on, instead of the pain in her heart.

Gemma woke a few hours later, in a great mood, but Claire was feeling too numb, closed to anything but the thought of Mark going to the press. Still, she managed to hide her fears and she and Gemma spent a quiet Sunday together, playing games, watching an old film on the television, and speaking on the phone to Lee and Cari.

'I hear you had a dinner guest last night.'

'Yes. We came home from town to find him sitting on the doorstep.' Claire kept her tone light, as if it had been a nice surprise, instead of one of the worst nights of her life.

'Mark was in the bar yesterday when I popped in. We had a nice little chat.'

Claire frowned. Fragments of her conversation with Mark began to filter into her mind.

'What about?'

'About the bar, and other things.'

Claire could well imagine what the other things were, but she did not feel inclined to get into another argument.

Her nerves were still frazzled from the night before.

'Do me a favour, Cari? If you happen to have another chat with him, leave me out of the conversation, please?'

Cari agreed lightly, wondering what had happened between Claire and Mark. But then Gemma came back on the line, and Cari had to be content with seeing Claire at work the next day.

Claire was trying to summon up enough courage to sit down and tell Gemma about Mark, but the moment never seemed right, and the next thing she knew, she was tucking Gemma in, and going downstairs for more time alone with her thoughts.

The next day, Claire kept up her pretence with herself, denying herself a spare moment to even think about Mark, and she busied herself with her work. She had staff meetings, a quick lunch with Cari, who, surprisingly, did not mention Mark at all, and a thousand other little jobs that she would normally have found tedious, but instead was grateful for, for the distraction they offered from her thoughts.

That was until she glanced at the clock and found it was time to leave to pick Gemma up from school. Where had the day gone? Claire had hoped that by filling her time completely, the day would drag, delaying the moment when she had to tell Gemma, but instead it had raced by and the moment was approaching like a speeding bullet. Her nerves instantly a mess, Claire managed to spill her cup of coffee all over a stack of papers on her desk, and Lee, walking past the open door, stepped into the office to see a flustered Claire trying to mop up the coffee whilst putting everything away.

'Everything okay?' he asked, with a smile.

'Huh?' Startled, she looked up with wide eyes, and then her features relaxed into a lop-sided smile, as she wiped away the rest of the coffee. Her hair had fallen partially from the neat French pleat she wore for work, and her cheeks were flushed. 'Yes, fine, thanks Lee. I'm leaving now to go and get Pip.'

Lee raised an eyebrow in surprise. 'What about Cari?'

'I thought I'd take her to see this film she's been going on about. We never had time over the weekend, and the last show is at three-thirty.'

'She'll like that,' Lee said.

'I hope so! We had a bit of a falling out on Saturday. She wanted to buy up the whole of Newcastle and I wasn't really in the mood for shopping!' Claire pulled a wry face and was relieved when Lee laughed.

'Well, have a good time, and have some popcorn for me. On the rare occasions Cari and I set foot in a cinema, she refuses to let me have any. Says it's fattening!' Lee patted his rounding stomach, and left the room chuckling to himself.

As Claire pulled up at the school, Gemma was saying goodbye to her friends. When she looked around for the familiar figure of Cari, she saw instead her mother. With a smile, she ran the short distance between them, and hugged Claire.

'Mum! What's wrong?'

'Why should anything be wrong?' Claire asked breezily, as she relieved Gemma of her school bag and a painting she had created lovingly that afternoon.

'Nana Cari always gets me!' Gemma skipped happily alongside her mother as they went to the car.

'I thought we could go and see that film at the cinema.' Claire unlocked the doors, and Gemma climbed in.

'The one with the dog and the cat?'

Gemma's excited tone made Claire smile as she took her place behind the steering wheel.

'That's the one. Do you want to see it?'

'Please!'

It was not until they were seated in the movie theatre, stocked up with bags of popcorn, and sweets, and huge cups of fizzy drinks, and the lights went down ready for the film to begin, that Claire's thoughts came back to Mark again. She remembered that he had mentioned seeing a lawyer, and made a mental note to go and see her own lawyer in the morning to find out exactly what claims Mark had on her daughter, if any. Before she knew it, the movie was over and Gemma was excitedly relaying her favourite parts as they walked the short distance to the fast food restaurant, where they were soon devouring hamburgers and fries.

Claire had ordered herself some food, but had not been planning on eating it. The churning of her stomach was so intense, she was sure that she would never keep it down. Once the food arrived though, she discovered that she was very hungry, and was soon munching as if she had not eaten for days. She reasoned that she would need some sustenance to see her through the next traumatic hours, to help her cope with Gemma's reaction. After another trip to the counter to obtain a large ice cream sundae for Gemma, Claire steeled her nerves, and began.

'So, did you tell all of your friends about your new clothes today?'

Gemma nodded happily, with her mouth full of chocolate ice cream.

'Melissa wants to come home and see them. She says her mum never buys her nice clothes. She says I'm lucky to have a mum like you.'

Claire smiled wryly at the intended compliment. 'I'm sure Melissa's mother buys her things. Did you tell them about the rest of the weekend?'

'We had to write in our diaries what we done. I wrote about my clothes, and about the game we played.'

'Nothing else? Nothing about Mark?'

'Nope.' Gemma was trying to lick ice cream from her chin. Claire handed her a napkin.

'Why not, Pip? Didn't you like him coming over?'

''Course I did. It's a secret, that's all!' she said, as if that explained it all.

'Who is it a secret from?'

'It's my secret. If I tell everyone, they'll want to see him. And he's mine!'

Claire closed her eyes at the fierce possessiveness in Gemma's voice. She hoped it wasn't going to change her normally happy-to-share daughter.

'I see.' She looked at her daughter.

'Is Mark coming over tonight?'

'No. Remember he's very busy, Pip. He has lots of other things to do.'

'I know, but he says he likes seeing me.'

So he had been working on her. Gemma was under his spell already, and Claire knew that by the end of the evening, she would be his completely. How was Claire supposed to cope with this? She had never before felt so possessive towards her daughter, had always shared her with Cari and Lee, but now she felt as though it was going to tear her heart in two to have to share Gemma's love with Mark.

After a minute of silence, Claire made her move.

'Pip, do you ever miss having a daddy?'

Gemma looked at her, a wistful look in her grey eyes, and Claire's heart twisted.

'Sometimes.' She looked down at the ice cream forming a sticky mess in the bottom of her dish. 'But you said you love me enough for a mummy and a daddy.' Gemma seemed to be waiting for confirmation.

Claire nodded. 'I do. Would you like to have a daddy, though?'

'Yes.' Gemma drew out the word, wondering whether or not that was the right answer. 'Only if you don't mind.'

Oh, but I do, sweetheart, more than you'll ever know, Claire thought to herself, but put a smile on her face.

'Remember I told you about your daddy? That we were in love, but some things happened and I had to go away?'

Gemma nodded.

'Well,' Claire paused to take a deep breath, praying that she could get through this with her heart in one

138

piece, 'your daddy is back.'

'You said you were the one who had to go away.' Gemma looked confused, and Claire realised it was going to be harder than she thought.

'Okay. I should have said that your daddy has found us.'

'He's here?' Gemma looked around, her little face turning red with excitement.

'No, darling. Not right now. But he wanted me to tell you about him.'

'Can I see him?'

Claire took another deep breath. 'If you like.'

'Now?' Gemma's eyes were sparkling, and her colour heightened.

'Soon.'

'What's his name, Mum?'

The hustle and bustle of the restaurant seemed to fade to silence, as Claire watched her daughter looking at her expectantly. There was a brief moment when Claire saw Gemma's soul in her eyes, and she almost gave way to the tears she was holding back. What if

Gemma suddenly decided that she preferred Mark to her? What if the little girl decided that she hated her mother for not telling her sooner about her father? What if she decided in later years that she resented her mother's selfishness and wanted nothing to do with her, just as Claire felt about her own mother? Whatever Gemma would feel, Claire knew it would not compare to the pain she would suffer at the hands of the press, and so she said the words that would bind her to Mark forever, no matter how she felt about him.

'His name is Mark, sweetheart. Mark Crofts is your daddy.'

5

Gemma's silence in the car as Claire drove home worried her. In the restaurant when she had spoken those fateful words, Gemma's face had paled then reddened again with a higher colour than Claire had ever seen.

'Mark?' Gemma had squeaked, and then had announced loudly that she felt sick. Claire had bundled the little girl out of the restaurant, concerned about her reaction. Anyone watching the scene might have deduced that Gemma had just eaten far too much ice cream.

Claire glanced at Gemma, the fleeting light of a street lamp showing that her colour had subsided slightly, but there was a strange look in her eyes that made her wonder if she had done the right thing. She had never been one of those over-protective mothers, but all she wanted to do now was to hide her away from Mark, from the threat of the press, and keep her safe.

'Are you all right, Pip?'

Gemma turned to look at her mother as if she had only just realised that they were not in the restaurant.

'Are we going home?' she asked, in a faraway voice that matched the look in her eyes.

'Yes, darling. Are you still feeling sick?'

'I don't think so. My tummy feels funny. Like bubbles.'

Claire gave her a relieved smile, hoping that it was only a case of mild indigestion brought on by too much fizzy drink, ice cream and excitement.

She stayed silent as she negotiated the car into her driveway, then turned to look at Gemma after she had parked the car in the garage. The gloom of the unlit garage filled the car, and Claire could only just make out Gemma's face.

'Is Mark really my daddy?' she asked.

'Yes, he is. How do you feel about that?'

'I don't think my tummy likes it much!' Gemma held her stomach as it growled.

Claire's laughter made her smile. 'Let's go and fix your tummy, and then we can see how the rest of you feels, okay?'

As soon as they shut the front door behind them, the phone began to ring in the kitchen. Normally, Gemma would have run to answer it, but she hesitated and looked at her mother. Claire smiled.

'I'll get it. It's probably Nana Cari wanting to know if we enjoyed the film.'

Claire hoped that was who it was, but as she picked up the receiver, she knew different.

'Where the hell have you been?' Mark's voice barked down the phone, causing Claire to flinch.

'We've been out,' she replied evenly, trying to keep her anger at Mark's tone under control.

'I know that. I've been phoning all afternoon. I'm sick to death with hearing your answerphone. Where have you been?' he asked again.

'We went to the cinema. I didn't realise that I had to report my every move to you!' Her tone was biting, and when Mark next spoke, he tried to pacify her.

'I was worried that you'd bolted again. You have a nasty habit of doing that.'

'Well, I didn't, so you can stop worrying. Gemma and I had a nice time, thank you for asking.' Claire smiled at Gemma, who had realised by that time that it was Mark.

'Did you tell her?'

'Yes.'

'How did she take it?'

'She says she feels sick to her stomach, if you must know!'

Mark's muttered curse, and Gemma's questioning look made her add, 'She ate too much popcorn at the pictures, and then stuffed her face with ice cream at the restaurant afterwards. Other than that, she seems to be okay.'

'Is she there now?' he asked.

'Yes, she's here.'

'Can I talk to her?'

Mark heard a short, muffled conversation the other end, as Claire covered the mouthpiece with her hand, then Gemma took the phone, pausing only to ask her mother what she should call him. Claire shrugged.

'Hello.' The little girl's voice sounded quiet.

'Hey, Pip! How are you?'

'Good. How are you?'

'I'm fine. Your mum tells me you just pigged out. Was it good?'

Gemma giggled. 'Yeah. I ate chocolate ice cream.'

'My favourite!'

'Mine too!' Gemma grinned.

'So did your mum tell you about me?'

'Yes.'

'And what do you think?'

'I told you that I wished you was my daddy.'

Mark remembered her murmured

words from the night before, and said softly, 'I'm glad.'

Claire watched as Gemma smiled and wondered what Mark was telling the little girl, what promises he was making that would soon be broken. Her thoughts wandered momentarily to her own broken heart and then she realised Gemma was saying goodbye.

'Okay, 'bye Daddy.' Gemma took the phone from her ear and held it out to Claire. 'Daddy wants to talk to you now.'

Claire took the proffered thing and shooed Gemma out of the kitchen. 'Yes?'

'Thank you,' was all he said, and the softness of his tone took her aback.

'For what?' she stammered, unnerved.

'For telling our daughter about me.'

The word 'our' jarred in Claire's mind, denoting a possession that she wasn't ready to grant him yet.

'I didn't have much choice in the matter, did I?' she snapped.

Mark's tone changed. 'I'm leaving to

come over now. I want to spend some time with her.'

That self-righteous presumption again. 'No. She's tired, and she needs an early night. I know what's best for her, and at this second, you're not it. You can come over tomorrow, if you like. She finishes school at three, and we'll be home just after that.'

'Claire . . . '

'Goodbye, Mark.'

She slammed the phone down, but she was shaking like a leaf, despite her strong words. Gemma poked her head around the door.

'Is Daddy coming over?'

'Tomorrow, Gemma. Tonight, you and I are going to have a talk about all of this,' Claire said firmly as she marched her upstairs to have a bath.

Gemma gibbered away about all the things she wanted to do with Mark, and all the things she wanted to show him, but when the little girl gave Claire a soap-sudded hug, all of the fight went out of her. More heartfelt hugs and kisses of love and appreciation were Claire's before she finally got Gemma to sleep, and just as Mark had done the night before, she sat in the chair, for hours, watching her sleeping daughter, wondering if things would ever be the same again.

Claire knew for sure the next day, when she came from visiting one of the company lawyers who dealt with all of Lee's legal matters. Claire explained her situation briefly to Russell Simmons, one of the senior partners in the law firm, Anderson, Simmons and Young, without giving away names and precise circumstances. She knew that if anyone got wind of her past relationship with Mark, they could go straight to the press, and that was definitely not what she wanted.

'So this man is your daughter's father?'

'Yes. I had a relationship with him seven years ago.'

'Were you married?'

'No, we weren't. We were living in sin.' A smile twisted her lips, and there was bitterness in her voice.

'Either way, you're no longer together.'

'No. I left him before I had Gemma.'

'And whose name is on the birth certificate? As the child's father I mean.'

'His.' Claire looked at him, concerned when he did not speak for a long moment. His chin was perched on templed fingers as he studied the notes he had taken. Finally, she could not stand the silence anymore.

'Well? Does he have any claim on her?' she snapped.

Russell gave her a long glance. He had dealt with enough people in this kind of situation to know when someone was scared of the answer, and Claire was more scared than most.

'I'm afraid so. If he is named as the child's father, then he has every right to access. He is also responsible legally for things like medical care, clothing, shelter, and so on.'

'I don't want his money. I just want to know if he can take her away from me.'

There was a hysterical tone to her voice, as she leaned towards him across the desk.

'If it were to go to court, there's a possibility that the judge could award joint custody with the father.' Upon seeing Claire's eyes close briefly, he continued, 'However, we would have to take into consideration other factors. You said you have brought the child up on your own so far?' He referred to his notes. 'Yes. The judge would consider the moral turpitude of the father, his standard of living, etcetera.'

'Standard of living,' Claire repeated faintly. Her cosy three bedroom house was sure to look like a hovel next to the sort of property Mark could afford with his millions. The room began to swim.

'Are you all right, Miss Montague?' Russell rounded the large oak desk in a second, and placed a hand on Claire's arm to steady her as she stood up.

'Yes, I'm fine. Thank you for talking me through it all. You've helped me make a few decisions.'

As she drove back to Stars, Claire's thoughts were on her daughter. It wasn't fair. It didn't matter to anyone that she was the one who had changed all her dirty nappies, suffered interminable sleepless nights when she was teething, given her all the love she could when there was no one else to chase away the monsters that lurked under her bed in the night.

Claire's mind was still in a fugue when she walked into her office, where she found a note from Rachel, her secretary, saying Gemma's school had phoned. Apparently there had been some kind of incident, and Gemma was now lying down in the nurse's office. Claire's heart was hammering as she sat at her desk and dialled the school's number with shaking fingers.

'Ridgemede Primary School. Can I help you?' said the school secretary answering the phone.

'Hello. This is Claire Montague, Gemma's mother. I had a message from the school about her.'

'Yes, Miss Montague. I'm afraid Gemma's a little upset after an incident at playtime. We wondered if you'd like to come and collect her. It's nothing too serious, so don't worry.'

'I'll be right there.'

Claire hung up just as Lee entered her office.

'That was the school. They want me to collect Gemma. She's upset about something.' Claire stood up and slung her handbag over her shoulder, whilst picking up her car keys. 'I'm sorry, Lee. I'll come straight back.'

'Don't be silly. Get Pip and go home.'

At the school, Claire entered through the main doors and knocked on the secretary's office door.

'Come in!' a woman's voice called, and Claire entered.

'Hello Miss Montague. I'm sorry you've had to leave work,' Mrs. Halligan smiled. 'Please, won't you sit down.'

Claire did. 'What happened?'

'Let me just go and fetch Gemma's teacher. She wanted to have a quick word with you first.'

The older woman left Claire in the small office, returning shortly with Mrs. Armstrong, Gemma's teacher.

'Good afternoon, Miss Montague.' Mrs. Armstrong extended her hand as she took a seat nearby.

'Mrs. Armstrong. What's the problem with Gemma? She's not in trouble, is she?' Claire could not imagine what kind of mischief her six-year-old could have conjured up that would warrant an immediate meeting with her teacher.

'Not at all. The children had to stay inside today at playtime, and there was a little scuffle between Gemma and another girl.'

Claire frowned. 'She didn't hurt the other girl, did she?'

'No.'

'So what was the argument about?'

Mrs. Armstrong looked pained, and pursed her lips before she spoke. 'I asked the other children what they had been fighting over, and they said that Gemma was telling them about her father, Mark Crofts.'

Claire sighed. She could imagine how this had played out.

'We all know who Mark Crofts is, and we all know that it can't be true. I know that you are a single parent, Miss Montague, but I wondered if you were aware that Gemma was inventing a father figure for herself? I'm afraid her friends weren't very understanding, and they told her she was a liar. Gemma was very upset.'

Claire closed her eyes briefly, then realised that Mrs. Armstrong was waiting patiently for a reply.

'Mrs. Armstrong,' she began with a smile, 'I do apologise for Gemma's little outburst this morning. You see, I broke off my relationship with Gemma's father before she was born, and he has only just now come back on the scene, so to speak.'

'Oh!' The other woman looked surprised. 'And is Gemma having difficulties accepting the situation?'

'No, she's not having any difficulty. The truth is, Mrs. Armstrong, that Mark Crofts is actually her father.' Claire noted with satisfaction that the teacher looked gobsmacked, for want of a better phrase. 'Obviously, it's not an ideal situation, what with him being so famous, but it's one we have to deal with. Gemma is just so proud of him that she wanted to tell her friends.'

'But, how . . . ?' Mrs. Armstrong's disbelief showed in her voice, and Claire remembered the self-assurance she always heard in Mark's voice, and drew upon it, pretending that she, too, was not used to having her words doubted.

'Clearly, it goes without saying that I'd like this to be between you and I, and of course, Mrs. Halligan.' Claire smiled kindly at the secretary who had been trying hard not to listen to the conversation, but was now looking at Claire with a mixture of awe and admiration.

'Of . . . of course, Miss Montague.' Mrs. Armstrong stammered, looking as if she had been knocked for six.

At that moment, Claire wished more than anything that she had made herself have that talk with Gemma last night, instead of putting it off, not wanting to spoil her happiness. Now, thanks to her soft-heartedness, and thanks to Mark's bloody well-known name and image, Gemma had already been hurt, and Claire felt as guilty as hell. But she wasn't about to shoulder the blame for this one altogether. She would have some choice words to say to Mark that evening, to set out the boundaries of his relationship with Gemma.

Mrs. Armstrong returned to her class, and Mrs. Halligan showed Claire to the nurse's office, where she found Gemma lying on the bed, reading a comic.

'Hey, baby!' Claire greeted her daughter softly, and Gemma sat up, with a brave smile, although her eyes filled with tears as soon as she saw her mother. 'Everything's alright,' she said, hoping against hope that it would be.

Gemma managed to hold onto her tears until they were in the car, but then the dam broke, and Claire's heart ached for her daughter as she sobbed in her arms. For a long time, the little girl could not speak, but eventually, the tears stopped and she was able to sit up, sniffing pitifully.

'They were horrible to me, Mummy. They said that Mark wasn't my daddy.' Gemma looked to her mother for reassurance, and it was there in Claire's smile.

'Of course he is, Pip. It's just that for a long time, you haven't had a daddy, and now you do, it's going to take a bit of time for everyone to get used to it. And not everyone is going to believe you when you tell them that Mark is your daddy.'

'Why not?' Gemma demanded.

'Because of who he is. Your daddy is very famous, Pip, and lots of people like him, just like you did before you knew he was your dad.' Claire stroked Gemma's hair from her tear-dampened face, as she explained patiently. Gemma thought on this for a while, and then smiled as if she had struck gold.

'Maybe Daddy can come to school and I can show everyone!'

'Maybe,' she agreed, as she started the car. 'You'll have to ask him tonight.' Smiling at the image of Mark and a classful of kids, she belted Gemma in. 'You have to promise me something though, Pip. Let's not tell anyone else about Daddy for the time being.' Claire put her finger to her lips. 'Let's make it our secret.'

Gemma nodded enthusiastically, pleased to have such an important secret, and put her own finger to her lips. 'Can I tell Nana Cari and Grandpa Lee? They like Daddy, Nana Cari told me!'

I bet she did, Claire thought, wondering what else she had told Gemma, and Mark for that matter. 'Yes, you can tell them, but then that's it, okay? Promise?'

'I promise!'

Once they were home, Claire insisted that Gemma go and lie down for a while, and despite her protests, when Claire checked on her half an hour later, the little girl was fast asleep. Finding herself with time on her hands once more, the afternoon seemed to stretch in front of her forever.

As she flitted aimlessly around the lower floor of the house, Claire let her mind wander, looking at photographs and ornaments and keepsakes that she had acquired over the years, and thought about everything that she had achieved since she came to Newcastle. She had been just nineteen years of age, with not enough money to live on, too much pain to live with, and nowhere to actually live. She'd had no clue as to what she wanted to do with her life, but she had scoured the local newspaper as she sat at the train station, and Lou's Lounge had been the first place she had tried. Lee and Cari had taken her into their lives and their hearts, and although the first few weeks had been difficult for her, Claire soon settled in.

Claire had rented a small bedsit upon her arrival but when Gemma was born, she found it hard to cope on her own and in such cramped conditions. When Cari offered her a room in their home, Claire accepted gratefully. For the first two years of her life, Gemma had three adults catering to her every need and was a very happy baby.

When Lee promoted Claire to assistant bar manager at Lou's Lounge, and then subsequently gave her more responsibility over the whole bar, she had saved enough money to buy a cottage in a small village about ten minutes from Lee and Cari's house. The cottage had been empty for a year when Claire and Gemma moved in and it had taken a lot of work to get it exactly how she wanted it. She could remember two-year-old Gemma 'helping', getting paint everywhere but on the walls; but with Lee and Cari pitching in, it was soon finished.

Claire looked around the living room, where she had come to a standstill, her fingers resting on the mantelpiece over the fireplace. There were pictures of Gemma everywhere, along with pictures of Lee and Cari. It's funny, she thought, how she had come to think of them as her family. Her own family, her mother and sister, had long since ceased to exist for her, ever since her father had died. A mild twinge of regret ran through Claire as she remembered how important her own father had been to her, and she wondered if Mark would mean the same to Gemma.

Over the past few days, Claire had been torn between thoughts of life with and without Mark as Gemma's father. Deep down, Claire still felt that if Gemma had never found out about Mark and vice versa, then they would have never have known what they were missing. But that was no longer an option, especially considering how Gemma felt about her father. Claire knew all she could do was try and keep her daughter safe, shielding her as much as possible from Mark's lifestyle, and the constant media attention that went along with it — and safe from a broken heart when Mark inevitably tired of her.

Claire tried not to compare Mark to her own father, because Mark would come up short every time. To her, Luke Mitchell was everything Mark Crofts was not. Luke had been a private person, preferring a quiet home life, and shying from the media attention that his wife's career had brought into their lives. He was warm and giving, honest and trustworthy, all the qualities that Mark was lacking as far as Claire was concerned. She wasn't sure that Mark could offer Gemma the things a child needed most: time and love. His career just did not allow for that.

'Why did you have to push it, Mark?' Claire asked out loud, anger in her voice at the turmoil he had created.

'Why the hell did you have to disrupt my life?'

The anger began to seep into her veins, and soon it was simmering, getting closer to boiling point. And at that moment, Mark rang the doorbell.

'Is she alright?' He did not wait to be invited in as Claire opened the door. 'I went by Stars,' he was saying and Claire watched him with an ever-deepening frown, 'and Lee told me you had to fetch Pip home early from school.'

Claire was seething and she felt like her head was going to explode.

'Daddy!'

The pair of them turned to see Gemma running down the stairs, and she threw herself into Mark's arms. Claire's heart cracked as she watched Mark wrap his arms around the little girl, and listened to his tender words. Uttering a stifled noise, she wheeled out of the room, neither father nor daughter noticing her departure.

In the kitchen, she crashed around making dinner, and realised that her one place of calm and safety, her own home, had become an emotional battleground for her. How dare he make all these demands on her time, when she didn't even want him there in the first place?

She was banging crockery and cutlery onto the table as Mark and Gemma entered the room. She had not told them dinner was ready, but Gemma could smell the food and had informed Mark that they should go and sit down. Only Mark seemed to be aware of the dark frown that was on Claire's face, and as he and Gemma noisily washed their hands at the kitchen sink, he cast a long look in Claire's direction. She was busy at the stove, her cheeks red from the steam from the pots, her hair damp around her face, the frown still knitting her brow.

Claire was unaware of Mark's perusal, and when she eventually sat down to eat, after making sure that everyone was served and happy, she was surprised to see a flicker of warmth in his eyes as she met his gaze. An unexpected warmth spread through her in answer, and it must have shown in her eyes, because Mark raised his glass of water to her before putting it to his lips. Claire flushed at the mock salute, angry with herself once more for being taken in by him. She fumed in silence throughout the meal, but Mark and Gemma's happy chatter filled the room.

Claire looked at Gemma as Mark filled her plate up with seconds, and could not help but be astounded at the change in the little girl in such a short space of time. It had not been more than five hours earlier when Gemma had been in tears, almost inconsolable, and here she was, smiling and laughing, as if she didn't have a care in the world. Claire acknowledged that, right at the moment, she didn't have. She knew that children were very resilient, but would Gemma be able to bounce back as quickly should Mark tire of the novelty of his new daughter? Claire pondered this thought for a while, and looked up in surprise when Mark told Gemma that maybe her mother would like to put her to bed tonight.

Claire's thoughts were with Mark all the while she was bathing Gemma, and even when she was reading her bedtime story. It was Gemma's favourite story, Sleeping Beauty. Gemma was in love with the idea that Prince Charming had come to the rescue. It had been one of Claire's fantasies as a little girl too, that she would fall in love with her own Prince Charming, someone who was exactly like her own father. After the heartbreak of losing her father, Mark had seemed to be the one to rescue her from that pain, but in the long run, he had only broken her heart again.

Gemma was asleep before Claire had even finished the book. At least Gemma's heart was safe whilst she was sleeping. Claire went back downstairs. Mark was not in the lounge, and when she opened the kitchen door, she found that room empty too. But there was a bottle of wine already opened on the table, with two glasses full. Claire's vain hope that Mark might have already left was dashed. With a heartfelt sigh, she took a seat, and suddenly feeling deathly tired, she put her arms on the table and lowered her head.

The sound of the door opening made her look up. Mark was standing at the end of the table watching her. Claire did not bother to meet his eyes, for she was sure that she knew what would be there: the same smugness she had seen before. She did not have the energy to deal with that. She picked up one of the glasses and took a long drink. The alcohol worked quickly, and she felt lightheaded. She did not realise that Mark had come to stand behind her until she heard him speak softly.

'You look absolutely shattered.'

Claire did not even give a sign that she had heard him and jumped when she felt his hands on her shoulders. If she was tense before, her muscles bunched even tighter at his touch. His hands were making slow, strong circles over her upper back, and despite herself she began to relax. Claire's mind began to wander as Mark's hands worked over her shoulders and when he touched the sensitive skin on the back of her neck, an unexpected sigh escaped from her lips. She was feeling more content at that moment than in many days, and did not feel inclined to move out of reach of this man.

Mark's fingers reached Claire's arms and she experienced a sudden flame of feeling in her lower belly, and opened her eyes quickly. What was he doing to her? She shouldn't be feeling like this. This was the man who had interjected himself into her life, and who might take her daughter from her. While these thoughts ran through her mind, her body was reacting to Mark's touch, and as his hand stroked her hair, a shiver of need went through her entire body.

It had been so long since she had been touched like that. Although she had ignored the part of her that needed intimacy over the last seven years, she had to admit that she had missed it. Mark removed his hands suddenly, and she looked at him wide-eyed as he knelt beside her chair. Her mind was in a haze of forgotten emotion, and his touch had a soporific effect on her body.

'I know it's been hard for you.'

Claire heard his words but was intent on the movement of his lips. She was remembering how they had felt when he had murmured words of passion, kissing her.

'I just wanted to say thank you, again.'

Claire made herself look into his eyes. The two of them were close and the flame burned brighter in her belly.

'For what?' she muttered, too entranced with his closeness to pay attention to the alarm bells that were ringing in her mind.

'For letting me spend time with Gemma. For letting me be here.'

Claire swallowed as she realised his face was coming towards her. She could see the intent in his eyes, just as she had seen it many times before.

'Let me in,' he whispered. 'I can make it all right, Claire!'

Her eyes closed as his lips gently touched hers. Claire found herself swept away by powerful feelings of need and desire. How could she have forgotten what it felt like to be kissed by this man? Her lips were tingling. She wondered how she had spent so long on her own.

Her back arched slightly, and Mark slipped one arm around her slender waist, and cupped her head with the other. He deepened the kiss, and Claire answered with a soft sound from deep within.

'I want you, Claire,' he muttered, his breath ragged, as he pressed tiny kisses to her throat. 'Please — I've got to have you.'

Claire jerked back, with a harshly uttered denial. She did not see Mark lose his balance and almost fall to the floor as she pushed the chair away from the table, causing both glasses of wine to topple and spill.

'What's wrong?' Mark exclaimed, as he hurried to the sink to get a cloth to mop up the spilled liquid.

Claire had backed herself against the cooker and stood shaking her head to try and clear the thoughts she had been having whilst Mark was kissing her. She had let him touch her, kiss her, and all the while she had enjoyed it. What was she thinking? It had been those last words that had snapped her out of her passion-filled reverie.

He honestly thought that he was going to possess her once more, just like that, just because she had weakened for a moment? She was angry at him for taking advantage of her when she was tired and feeling weakened by the emotional stress of the past few days, but she was furious at herself for letting her guard down around him for even one second. She knew what he was like, how he used people, and expected to have everything he wanted, immediately.

Claire's head had cleared by the time Mark threw the wet cloth into the sink and stood in front of her with his hands on his hips. Claire could see from the frown on his face that he was having difficulty understanding why she had torn herself from his embrace when for all the world she had appeared to be enjoying it. Well, she was more than ready to tell him.

'What's going on?' Mark voiced the question, and levelled a look at her.

Mark had already had his turn when he had threatened to go to the press if she did not tell Gemma about him. Now it was her turn.

'I'll tell you. You may have won the love of a little girl, but by no stretch of the imagination does that mean that I am included in the deal.'

'What?' Mark looked incredulous, as if he could not understand the words coming from her mouth. 'What do you mean?'

'I mean, Mark,' she said, her voice loud, 'that I want nothing to do with you. I may have been stupid enough to let you kiss me just now, but it is not going to happen again, do you hear me? I have had enough of you to last me a lifetime. I learned my lesson years ago when I walked in on you with that woman. You can deny it all you want,' she said, holding up her hand, as Mark began to shake his head, 'but I saw you with my own eyes.'

Mark stared at her angrily whilst she caught her breath. 'What woman?'

'The one you were entertaining in our flat. In our bed.'

She watched as his face turned pale, understanding dawning. 'When you fell down the stairs . . . It was after you saw us, wasn't it?' He hung his head. 'I was meant to be shooting a video,' he stammered. 'I'd got rather drunk and it got out of hand. Justin used some woman that had been hanging around for weeks. I knew what she wanted, what most groupies want, but I had you. We ended up kissing, but I swear to you, that's all it was. I'm so sorry Claire, I was such an idiot.'

'I can think of worse things to call you, but idiot will do.'

'I just hope you can find it in your heart to forgive me.' Mark looked like a kicked puppy and although she could forgive him, she wouldn't forget.

'You messed up any kind of future we might have had together. I didn't trust you then, and I most certainly don't trust the kind of man you've become!'

'And what kind of man have I become?'

Claire smiled wryly. He was making it too easy for her. If she held any kind of reservations about telling him to his face exactly what she thought of him, for fear of him doing something to hurt Gemma, they had vanished into thin air. She had seven years of pent up emotions to vent.

'You're arrogant, self-centered, spoiled,

rude and thoughtless. You waltz back into my life, demanding that I hand my daughter over to you on a plate. You blackmail me with the press, apparently without thinking about the consequences. Can you imagine how she would feel if she had her picture plastered across every single newspaper in the country? No, I don't suppose you can, because it's second nature to you, and you love every single minute of it, don't you?'

She didn't wait for his answer, she was on a roll. 'You have been her idol for a long time, but she hasn't reached the age yet where she can distinguish between you as her father and you as a rock star. I can, and I don't like what I see at all. Gemma is the only reason you're here, but if you step one foot out of line, if you mess up my daughter's life, then you will never see her again. We will disappear, just like we did before, and you won't find us. I promise you that, Mark.'

Claire finished, a brief thought crossing her mind that she might just have taken it a bit too far, but it did not settle. She had not expected silence from him and it was making her nervous. She watched him for the longest time, and when he opened his mouth to speak, she held her breath.

'We'll see.'

And with that, he left the kitchen, slamming the door behind him. Claire heard the front door slam so hard that she was sure she felt the house rocking in its foundations. She crumpled to the floor, dissolving in tears. Tears that she should have cried a long time ago, for now she knew that the man she had once loved no longer existed. There was not a single shred of compassion left in Mark, and it broke her heart. She sat on the kitchen floor, trying to hold both her heart and her life together with her two hands.

6

Claire kept Gemma home from school the next day, as she was running a temperature. As Claire telephoned the school secretary, she was sure that the fever had less to do with actually being ill than the prospect of spending the day with Mark. Claire's own temperature rose when she thought of him, but it was with a fierce anger that made her blood boil. She had told him in no uncertain terms the night before how she felt about his presence in her life, and whether her anger was directed at him for violating her home or at herself for letting him be there in the first place, it no longer mattered. She had set the limits for all three of them, and now she was going to have to make sure that no one crossed the line she had drawn in the sand.

Claire had to make sure that Gemma

did not become too attached to Mark, and that Mark himself did not abuse his new relationship with his daughter. Gemma had already been on the phone to her father that morning to tell him she was not going to be in school, wanting to know if he'd spend the day with her. Claire had spoken to him briefly and knew from the tone of his voice that he had indeed heard her words clearly the night before. He had been cool, but polite, and Claire came off the phone with a feeling of satisfaction.

That feeling deepened later in the day after Claire and Gemma had spent several hours in his company. They had gone to the local zoo, and the little girl had dragged Mark around to see all the animals. Claire had watched him closely, and not once had he stepped out of line. He had been affectionate with Gemma, but had avoided making any long-term plans with her. He had rarely looked at Claire, and she felt a sense of relief to be out of his sphere of attention. She was still feeling tender from the experience of having Mark kiss her, and did not trust her traitorous body near him.

She had spent many hours after Mark left, torturing herself with the recollection of his touch that evening, and of the thousands of times he had touched her like that before, hoping that she could somehow desensitise herself, but all it had done was make her senses even more aware of him. He had reawakened her sexuality with a touch, and it frightened her. Claire had tried to convince herself that she had backed away from him because she could not stand to be near him, but deep down, in the place where desire and need lived, she knew that was not the truth. She had pushed him away because she was scared of what might have happened, scared of the power he had over her. Hence, she was aware of his every movement as she watched him with Gemma, and she acknowledged that she still found him attractive

As they sat down to lunch in the zoo's empty cafeteria, Claire found Mark's eyes on her. He had not spoken to her for hours, but when Gemma went to the bathroom, he turned to face her.

'How am I doing?' he asked and Claire was surprised at the coolness in his voice. How fast he could switch! Just a few seconds before he had been laughing and joking with Gemma, and here he was now, looking at Claire as if he hated her. Her heart was beating fast as she stammered her words and she wondered where all this new found control of hers had scarpered.

'I . . . I don't know what you mean.' Claire poured herself a cup of tea, so that she did not have to look at him. Her hand was shaking so much that she spilt most of it on the table. Why was he having this effect on her?

'Still think I'm being self-centered and thoughtless?'

Mark was watching her through narrowed eyes, and Claire felt like she was under interrogation.

'I don't want to discuss this now,' she mumbled. 'I told you what I wanted from you, let's just leave it, okay?'

'I don't actually recall you telling me what you want, Claire. Instead, I heard a lot about what a terrible person I was, how I wasn't to be trusted, how I wasn't to do anything to hurt Gemma. Why don't you try again?' Mark threw her a patient look, and Claire knew he was mocking her.

'What I want, Mark,' she leaned across the table towards him, her trembling voice hardly above a whisper, 'what I really would like, is for you to disappear from my life, to pretend that you never found me again, to forget that you are Gemma's father. But that's not a possibility, is it?'

'No!'

'Then you can spend time with her; that's all. I don't want you around and I really wish that you had never found out about Gemma, but you have. I may not like the situation, but she comes first in all of this.'

Mark levelled a long hard look at her, and then Gemma came back and the moment passed. Claire was secretly relieved that she had escaped any further conversation with him, for she imagined there was a lot more he wanted to say to her.

They finished their drinks and left the restaurant, and Gemma's happy chatter filled the crisp air as they began to walk around the rest of the zoo. Claire was watching Mark like a hawk, ready to come down on him like a ton of bricks if he stepped one foot out of line.

If Mark thought that he was going to be the perfect father, without having had any experience of children in his life, then he was hugely mistaken. Claire had brought Gemma up to be polite and well-behaved, but, just like any child, she could play her mother up something chronic when she felt like it and have tantrums that could shock the hell out of someone who did not know her. And Mark did not know her.

Gemma would probably enchant him with her happy smiles, and she would wind him around her little finger, because that is what little girls do with their fathers. He would buy her things, because she asked him to, and because money was no object to him. Would he ever learn that money does not buy love, and that it certainly would never buy respect? Did he know that sometimes he would have to say no to her, and suffer the consequences, just like Claire had done on their shopping trip in Newcastle at the weekend?

Would Mark be able to cope with the rebellion and antagonism that was bound to come with a daughter, because Claire could already see it in Gemma sometimes, and it reminded her of herself when she had been younger. Claire smiled gently at the memory of her father being firm but kind with her. She had respected him for that.

Tearing herself away from her thoughts,

Claire could see that Gemma was getting tired. She was dragging her feet, her bottom lip beginning to pout, as Mark tried to get her interested in the meerkats. Gemma could be a handful when she was tired, and Claire grinned to herself — Mark would be stressed when Gemma started to act up. Claire would have almost enjoyed seeing Mark being hassled, but she was still a mother, and once again, concern for her daughter's welfare overrode anything else. She went to speak to Gemma.

However, Mark too had seen the pouting lower lip, and had smiled, because that was exactly what Claire used to do when she was tired. Almost laughing, he made a little game of chasing Gemma, who, by the time he caught her, and put her on his back, was laughing wildly, causing her mother to join in.

Mark looked at Claire, and although she stopped laughing almost instantly at his gaze, she could not take the smile from her face at seeing her daughter happy. She walked a little behind the two of them, as she began to alter her opinion of Mark's parenting skills. He was actually pretty good with the child, and seemed to be enjoying their time together.

Shortly, they came to the zoo's gift shop, and after Gemma's lust for clothes shopping at the weekend, Claire preferred to stay in the background and let Mark deal with this one. Claire was not sure if Gemma knew that Mark was wildly wealthy, but the little girl knew from all her friends who had divorced parents that when fathers came to visit, they got lots of presents. Claire wondered if this was how Gemma saw Mark.

Gemma loved cuddly toys, and this being a zoo, the shop had plenty to choose from. The little girl was in raptures over monkeys, giraffes, tigers and all sorts of exotic creatures. Claire was admiring some jewelry and smiled to see Mark being dragged all over the shop to look at one thing or another.

Having had enough, Mark pulled an excited Gemma to a halt in front of the cuddly toys, her eyes bright with the prospect of little goodies, and explained to her that she would have to choose one thing.

Claire raised an eyebrow at the stunned look on Gemma's face, waiting to see if she was going to start a tantrum, but Mark's soft voice had an authority to it that Gemma seemed to recognise, and after some half-hearted attempts at bargaining for maybe two or three, she nodded and set about choosing her single toy.

Mark joined Claire and let out a breath.

'You had a lucky escape there. She usually puts up more of a fight than that!' Claire couldn't help but laugh aloud.

Mark shrugged and grinned. 'I had visions of her having a paddy and chucking toys everywhere, trashing the shop, breaking all the glass!'

'What's the matter, scared you'd have

to pay for it all?' Mark looked unsure at her comment, but she smiled. 'Just teasing! You did alright!'

'Yeah?'

Claire found herself looking into Mark's eyes, then at his mouth . . .

'I want this one, Daddy!' Gemma announced, as she dragged a four-foot-high polar bear towards them, narrowly missing a display of crystal ornaments.

'Please!' Claire muttered, as she rescued the bear, thankful of the distraction, and ashamed of the way her thoughts had just behaved, hoping that Mark had not noticed the way her gaze had lingered. But as she reached the counter, and he helped her haul the monstrous bear up for the cashier to see the price, his hand touched hers, and the way he looked at her told her that he had indeed seen her reaction. Flustered, she made Gemma thank her father for the present, and was relieved that Gemma's hugs and kisses on Mark's face hid her from his eyes, albeit momentarily.

It was getting dark outside as they made their way back to the Range Rover, carrying the huge toy between the three of them, although Gemma was more of a hindrance than a help as she alternated between Mark and Claire, holding their free hands whilst trying to hold the bear too.

Once again, the heat inside the vehicle once they were on their way sent Gemma nodding off. It was having a very relaxing effect on Claire too. Apart from when she had shared journeys with Lee and Cari, it had been a long time since she had been driven around by anyone, and it took her back to the time when she lived in London. She'd been very unsure about driving, given the fact that she hadn't long passed her test when she met Mark, and was not confident enough to negotiate the traffic. She'd also had a mild fear that she, too, would perish in an accident like the one that had taken her father from her. But she had always felt safe being driven by Mark.

She felt safe enough now, but she also felt strange — as if she was giving up a tiny piece of her independence. Claire glanced quickly at Mark's profile whilst he was negotiating a tight bend, and the earlier heat returned. She turned her head quickly to gaze out the window, but her thoughts stayed with him. How was it that he could have such an effect on her? One minute she was boiling over with venom towards him, and the next she was practically offering herself on a plate to him. What was going on?

Before Mark had turned up, Claire's life had been very consistent. There were no major events or upheavals, no peaks and troughs of emotion, just a calm and peaceful way of life; her and Gemma, with Lee and Cari. Claire had been comfortable with where she was in her life, she hadn't needed anyone else. And yet here she was, alternately repulsed by and wildly attracted to this man.

Over the last seven years, she had

dealt with the fact she was alone, and that she was over Mark. But when he'd turned up last week, all that had changed. He had thrown her world into turmoil and she was having difficulties adjusting to it.

How was it possible that she could still be attracted to him after all this time, and after she had seen him with that woman? Was she not of sound mind? Obviously not, the way her imagination had her limbs entwining with his.

'Stop it!' Claire whispered aloud, causing Mark to look at her questioningly.

'Stop what?' he asked, as they came to a halt at the traffic lights in the village where Claire lived.

'Oh, nothing! I was just thinking aloud.'

They passed the fish and chip shop, and she sniffed. 'Mmm!'

'How about we have chips tonight, instead of you cooking? That's all you seem to have done since I got here!' Mark suggested.

Apart from fight you every step of the way, Claire thought to herself. 'That's my lot in life, I'm afraid!'

'There's much more, Mitch,' he said quietly, as they pulled up outside the house. He got out of the car abruptly, leaving Claire wondering whether she had heard him right.

Claire took the bear and Mark carried Gemma and they entered the house. Gemma was sleepy for a short while, but was soon on the phone to Lee to tell him that she hadn't been to school today, and that they'd been to the zoo and she'd brought home a big polar bear.

'I hope it's not a real one, darling!' Lee laughed, glad to hear that they'd had a good time.

After having a quick word with Claire, who promised that she would be back to work tomorrow, the conversation ended and Mark and Gemma went down to the fish and chip shop to fetch dinner, leaving Claire alone with Icicle, as Gemma had named the stuffed toy.

Claire was just straightening up the lounge when she heard a phone ring.

Rushing to the kitchen, she realised that it wasn't hers. Her own mobile was switched off in the car, and she couldn't remember seeing Mark's, but then she spotted it on the table in the hall.

She stood by it, listening to it ring, not sure whether or not she should answer it. After having a furtive look around the hallway to make sure that there were no witnesses, she picked it up and answered.

'Hello?' she said quietly.

'Mark? Who is this?' an imperious, high-pitched, female voice came down the phone.

'Who is this?' Claire returned, not liking the woman's tone.

'I'm trying to reach Mark. I think I may have dialled the wrong number.'

'No, you haven't. This is his phone, but I'm afraid he's not here at the moment.' Claire had a feeling she recognised the woman's voice.

'What's he doing, and who are you?' There was what sounded like hysteria in her voice.

'He's getting dinner. I'm just a friend. Can I take a message for you?' Claire asked politely.

The woman on the other end of the phone faltered for a while and when she spoke again, her tone was more pleasant. 'I wonder if you could. It's quite important that I speak to Mark. I've been trying to get hold of him for days, but this is the first time his phone has been switched on.'

'No, you're quite right. He's been a bit busy, and he is supposed to be on holiday, so he left it off. Who shall I say called?'

'My name is Jennifer.'

'And your surname?' Claire knew damn well what it was.

'He'll know who I am, we're close friends.' A hint of smugness entered Jennifer's voice. Oh yeah, Claire thought, how close?

'Really?' She pretended to sound surprised. 'He's never mentioned you before. How long have you known him?' It wasn't a complete and utter lie,

Claire thought; Mark hadn't mentioned her once.

'About six months.' It sounded like all the air had gone out of Jennifer's sails, and Claire felt just a slight pang of guilt, remembering that Jennifer was only in her early twenties and probably very insecure, just like Claire's own sister had been at the beginning of her modelling career. But she twisted the knife anyway.

'Oh, right! Mark and I go back a long way. I've known him over ten years. That's probably why he hasn't mentioned you. When you've been close to someone for that long, you don't always need words to communicate.' Claire paused, satisfied to hear a slight noise from the other end of the line. 'Well, I'd better go now, dinner's almost ready. Nice talking to you, Jennifer. I'll mention to Mark that you called. 'Bye!'

With a malicious little grin, she hung up and set about getting the plates and cutlery ready. The doorbell rang then, and Claire let Gemma and Mark in, both of them red-faced from the cold.

'I'm starving!' Gemma announced dramatically, as she dragged herself out of her coat and practically ran into the kitchen, where Mark was already starting to dole out the food onto the plates.

Looking at Claire, he said, 'I realised when we got there that I hadn't asked you what you wanted, so I got you a pasty. You always used to like them!'

Claire nodded happily, having enjoyed her conversation with Jennifer. She was not normally one to be mean on purpose, but it had made her feel good. 'That's fine, a pasty is great!'

Mark paused momentarily, wondering why she was in raptures over a bit of pastry, but gave her an amused smile as he continued with the task at hand. Soon, they were all tucking into their food, happily chatting about the day, and Claire did not notice the questioning glances Mark was giving her.

After dinner, Claire took Gemma upstairs

for a bath while Mark was left to do the washing up, because 'he needed the practice'. They were enjoying a bubble-blowing competition when Mark joined them, perching on the toilet.

'Do you always make this much mess?' he laughed, surveying the water dripping down the side of the bath, and how soaked Claire was.

'Why do you think I've not put a carpet down?' Claire indicated to the varnished floorboards. 'She used to be a lot worse than this.'

'Mum used to have a bath with me, and she made more mess than me!' Gemma giggled, blowing bubbles into Claire's hair.

'You little monster!'

Mark left them to get on with it, listening to the noise as he walked down the stairs. As he reached the bottom, he recognised the ring of his mobile, and realised that Gemma must have left it switched on when she was playing with it earlier.

'Hello?'

'Mark? At last! It's Justin. Where the hell have you been? I've been ringing you for days.'

With a frown, Mark answered, 'I haven't had the phone switched on.'

'Don't you pick up your messages ever? Where are you anyway?'

'I'm in Edinburgh. Where else would I be?'

'Cut the crap, Mark! Your hotel in Edinburgh was the first place I tried. They said you haven't been near the place.'

'I'm staying with a friend, if that's okay with you, Justin. Now, did you have something important to say, because I'm kind of busy right now.'

Mark glanced at Claire as she came into the living room, and took a seat on the sofa.

'I've just had an hysterical call from Jennifer, if you must know,' answered Justin. 'It seems that she called your mobile and some woman answered.'

'What woman?' he asked slowly, watching as a slight blush appeared on

Claire's cheeks as she studied a magazine.

'How do I know? Jennifer didn't get her name, just that she was an old friend of yours. Is it someone I know? Is that who you're staying with?'

'It's got absolutely nothing to do with you where I am or who I'm staying with. Now, before you get on your high horse, can I remind you that I'm on holiday? That means I'm not working, and *that* means that I don't want to speak to you until I get back. So now I am going to turn this damn thing off, and leave it in the car. If I need to get in touch, I will. Thanks for calling. 'Bye!'

With a resolute poke of his finger, he turned the phone off and put it down on the table.

'I take it that was Justin. He's still with you then?' Claire raised blue eyes to meet his.

'Yes, although I really wish he wasn't sometimes.'

'How is the little weasel?'

'You've never liked him, have you?' Mark narrowed his eyes at her.

Claire shrugged. 'I have plenty of reasons not to, Mark. So what did he want, anyway?'

'Just to tell me that people have been trying to get hold of me.'

'Who?'

'Jennifer?' Mark posed it as a question, raising one eyebrow as he perched on the edge of the coffee table, his knees touching hers as she sat on the edge of the sofa.

'Oh, yeah!' Claire said, nonchalantly. 'I forgot to tell you, she phoned while you were out.'

'You forgot?'

'Yep! She didn't really leave a message, so I figured she'd phone back if it was important.'

'She phoned Justin instead, apparently almost hysterical.' Mark leaned towards her. 'What did you say to her, Claire?'

'Nothing much!' Claire tried to suppress a grin.

'Mitch?' He leaned dangerously close

to her, and her mouth produced a delightfully mischievous grin. She looked deep into his eyes, which were sparkling.

'Honestly, I didn't say much at all. Just that you were otherwise engaged, sorting dinner.'

'And?' he prompted, grinning himself, watching her closely.

'And she said you two were close friends, so I told her how long we had known each other. I think she got a bit upset!'

Mark was laughing now, and Claire's grin grew larger.

'Well, she shouldn't be phoning! You're on holiday!'

'Are you sure it was nothing proprietary?' Mark slid to the edge of the table so that one of his legs was between Claire's thighs, and placed one warm hand on her arm. She could feel the heat from his skin through her thin jumper. She watched as his hand lifted and gently brushed a strand of hair back from her face, all the while looking at her eyes, her lips. His fingers brushed her cheek, the lobe of her ear, her throat and then her lips, which parted without a second of hesitation.

His fingers were soon replaced by his own lips, already parted, eager to touch hers. Claire felt as though she was falling.

His hand moved from her arm to her hip, where it moved in tantalizing little circles, making her shiver, needful of closer contact, shifting restlessly under his hand, reaching for him with her own hands, fingertips flexing at the ripple of his muscles. At her touch, a soft noise came from Mark, giving Claire a delicious feeling of power over him, as age-old as the hills, making her want to hear more.

Then they heard the thump of Gemma coming down the stairs, and looked at each other. Mark had time to plant one more sensual, liquid kiss on her lips before their daughter entered the room, and he stood to pick her up and swing her round, giving Claire a moment to try and compose herself.

She smiled as she watched Mark playing with Gemma, remembering with heat in her belly the way they had kissed, but then her smile began to fade as she met his eyes. Gone was any of the passion that had been there just seconds before; all she could see was the metal grey she had encountered when they first met at the club.

She left the room unnoticed and went up to the bathroom to clear up the devastation left by Gemma.

As she scrubbed the bath with vigour, she schemed in her mind. If that was all he saw her as, then he was going to have the shock of his life. If Mark Crofts could switch his passion on and off like that, then she could too. If Mark Crofts saw her as a little distraction while Gemma was not around, then she could do the same.

Finishing, she threw the sponge into the corner of the bath, sat back on her heels, and exhaled deeply. Who was she kidding? She wanted him, no matter how much she tried to convince herself otherwise.

She stood up, angry with herself. She was turning into one of his little groupies, just like Jennifer. When she had first met Mark, his looks were not the most important thing to her. She had fallen in love with his gentleness, his kindness, and most of all, because he looked after her and made her feel safe.

Now, she was her own person; she didn't need anyone to look after her, least of all Mark Crofts. Damn him! Deciding that she needed some time on her own, she firmly locked the bath-room door and started to run a bath.

Only when she was fully immersed in the hot, bubble-filled water did she start to relax, letting her mind wander, feeling the pressure she had been under for what felt like an eternity, disperse with the bubbles as they began to pop.

Things might be okay, as long as she did not think any further ahead than the next day. Peaceful, Claire did not even hear the whispering outside the bathroom door.

Mark had decided to put Gemma to bed, without disturbing her. Instead, he helped Gemma write a note, which they slipped, unnoticed, under the bathroom door.

When the water had finally lost every vestige of heat, Claire reluctantly got out of the bath and let the water out. Locating a fresh towel and wrapping herself in it, she gathered up her clothes, and found the note on the floor. In Gemma's messy scrawl, it said:

Dear Mummy, Daddy said I should go to bed. I am in bed, and you are in the bath. Daddy is waiting for you downstairs. Goodnight, love Gemma xxx

With a smile, Claire left the bathroom, got changed into an old, but comfortable, grey tracksuit and went downstairs. The kitchen was dark, and upon hearing music from the lounge, she opened the door.

Mark looked up from his perusal of a pile of CDs next to him on the sofa. His eyes ran the length of her before he spoke.

'Hey, gorgeous!'

Claire blinked hard, unsure of what she'd heard. Wrinkling her nose, she perched on the arm of the sofa. 'What, in this? Your taste has gone downhill!'

'I don't think so! Besides, you've always looked good in whatever you've worn.'

'Yeah, like that outfit I wore to my eighteenth? That was hideous!' She was referring to an impulse buy from a trendy designer boutique in London, a monstrous creation of shiny red PVC, skin tight, in which she could hardly move, let alone dance or even drink much, because it was a nightmare trying to go to the toilet in it!

'I happen to think that was one of the sexiest things you've ever worn!' Mark grinned. 'Have you still got it?'

Claire laughed. 'It's probably upstairs somewhere. You know I don't like throwing things away!'

'Tell me about it. I can remember having to fight to find space to put everything away when we had that flat. But it's a habit I picked up when you went. I haven't had a good clear out in years.'

Claire looked uncomfortable at the mention of her leaving, and shifted in her seat.

'Why don't you come and sit here?' He patted the seat next to him.

Claire looked at him for a long moment. What was she doing? She couldn't get inside his head, she couldn't read his feelings, not like she used to; so instead, she offered to show him Gemma's baby pictures.

They spent an enjoyable hour looking at six years' worth of photos, and then Mark asked, 'Where are the rest of them? Your family, me and you?'

Claire shook her head. 'I put them away upstairs in the loft when we moved in. The ones of my family hurt too much to have around.'

'And the ones of us?' The question hung in the air.

'When Gemma started to be a fan of yours, I thought it would be a lot easier if she didn't see them, so she wouldn't ask questions.'

'Is that the same reason you never told her who her father was?' There was an edge to Mark's voice.

'That's different altogether!' She stood up, and looked at him. 'She knows now, and you know about her. Isn't that enough?'

'I don't know if it is, Claire. How do I know that when I have to go back to London, you're not going to do another runner?'

'What I said the other night — it was in the heat of the moment. I'm not about to leave my job and my home. I've made a life for myself here, Mark, and nothing is going to change that'

'And what if I were to ask you to come down and live with me in London?'

'You're mad!' Claire exclaimed. 'What the hell would I want to go back to London for? And what do you mean, live with you? I'm not leaving Newcastle, and neither is Gemma. If you need to, you can stay here when you want to see her, but that doesn't mean anything is ever going to happen between us!'

'What about earlier?' His voice was quiet after her little outburst.

'What about earlier? It was just a kiss. If you must know, you're the closest I've been to a man since I left London. I've been alone for seven years — by choice, I might add — and there you are all of a sudden, and I guess old memories die hard. A kiss, Mark, no more, and if you think you're going to get anything else out of me apart from Gemma, then you'd better leave this house right now!'

Mark stared at her and then, to her amazement, he stood up, picked up his phone and coat, and walked out the door.

7

Thursday was a dismal day, in more ways than one. Gemma had awoken Claire in the small hours, screaming her head off because a giant polar bear was coming to eat her. The only way to stop Pip's heebie-jeebies was for Claire to take her back into her own bed. This was not a productive move. For a little thing, Gemma took up as much room as any adult, if not two, and writhed and wriggled so much that Claire eventually found it easier to sleep in the spare room.

Waking up at first light, Gemma had hounded Claire out of bed, demanding to know where Mark was, what had she done to him, and was he ever coming back? Outside, it was pouring with rain, the sky dark and grey, matching the thunderous expression on Gemma's face on the way to school, muttering under her breath because Claire had tried to explain why Mark had not stayed.

'But mummies and daddies sleep in the same bed!' The little girl was adamant.

'Only if they are married, love, and Mark and I are not married,' Claire reiterated patiently.

Gemma looked at her mum, determined to have the last word, her hands clenched tightly as she tried to think of something to say. There was silence as Claire drew the car to a halt, and turned in her seat to face Gemma.

'Now, do you remember what we talked about the other day, Pip? About your dad being a secret?'

Gemma nodded sullenly, glaring at her mother.

'Don't be like that, sweetie!' Claire reached out to touch her daughter's cheek.

'You've been such a good girl the last few days, let's not ruin it now, eh?'

Gemma opened the door, and Claire

began to think that for the first time ever, she was going to walk into school without saying goodbye to her.

'Gemma?' Claire called, and leaned over the passenger side to try and catch her daughter's hand, barely brushing her fingertips.

Gemma snatched her hand away, and reeled round, her face red and angry. 'Then you got to marry him!' she almost shouted, and ran into the playground, leaving Claire open-mouthed.

She was dumbfounded all the way to work, where she told Lee what had happened, only for him to burst out laughing, the rumbles echoing around her office.

'It's not funny, Lee! It's bad enough that I have to put up with Mark's presence because he's Gemma's father, but to expect me to marry him?' Lee went into further paroxysms at the indignant look on Claire's face, until even she began to see the funny side of the situation.

The morning flew by as Claire fell

211

back into a working rhythm, and as she took a taxi to meet Cari at the bar for lunch, the sun was starting to come out.

'Hello, love!' Cari greeted her with a warm hug. 'How are you?' She held the younger woman at arm's length to get a proper look at her. 'You look like you've lost weight. Aren't you eating properly? Or are you worried about your appearance now that hunky boyfriend of yours is back on the scene?' Cari grinned.

'Do you mind? I've got you passing Mark off as my boyfriend and Gemma trying to marry us off so that we can sleep in the same bed!'

Cari laughed as they walked inside.

'I don't know whether I'm coming or going these last few days, Cari. Between the pair of them, they have me climbing the walls.'

'Let's get you a drink and then you can tell me all about it.' Cari ushered Claire to the table, while she went and sorted the drinks out.

Sitting down, Claire remembered Mark walking out the door last night, to her complete and utter surprise. She certainly hadn't expected him to leave. Did that mean that he was too disgusted to even think about being with her like that, or that it was exactly what he had expected? With a sigh, she took the cappuccino that Cari offered her, and took a sip.

'So, how is it going with you two, then? Seems Gemma really likes him.' Cari looked at Claire over the rim of her cup. Claire frowned slightly.

'It's going as well as you'd expect, for someone seeing the father of her child for the first time in nearly seven years, and finding her life completely out of control.'

Cari raised an eyebrow. She could see that Claire was mildly agitated, and wondered if it was because of Mark. She could not think of any other reason. 'And you don't like being out of control, do you, Claire?'

'Of course I don't!' Claire exclaimed.

'Who does? He waltzes back into my life and expects me to drop everything, just for him. The nerve of the man!' Claire paused to take a sip of her coffee. Warming to her subject, and grateful to have someone to talk to after having chased herself around in circles the last few days, she continued, 'I don't know what he wants from me, Cari, I honestly don't. Sometimes I think he's here just for Gemma. He's so natural with her, and I think he's starting to love her. But then, the next minute, he's either looking at me as though I'm something he's stepped in, or like he wants to drag me into bed!'

Claire paused to think of that particular scenario, a tiny smile playing at the corner of her mouth, and then flushed guiltily as she caught Cari looking at her with a knowing smile.

'What?' she mumbled, trying to hide her red face in her coffee cup.

'You don't seem too upset with that last option. Could it be that you are ever-so-slightly still in love with him?'

'No! I'm not a child anymore, I'm over having little schoolgirl crushes, thank you very much.'

'Oh, come on!' Cari laughed. 'You can't tell me that you don't find Mark even the slightest bit attractive. I wouldn't believe you anyway. If I was a few years younger and hadn't met my Lee . . . '

Claire tried to suppress her smile, but it didn't work. 'Of course I find him attractive, but he's so much in love with himself, he doesn't need anyone else's encouragement.'

'Rubbish! He has to have some kind of attitude when he's performing, but when you meet him in the flesh, he is very down to earth. And what flesh!'

'You are wicked, Mrs. McGuire!' Claire laughed, causing Cari to join in.

'May I ask what's so funny?' a male voice asked, and both women turned to see Lee, followed by Mark, approaching them.

'Just girls' stuff, darling!' Cari kissed Lee. 'Hello, Mark. How are you?'

'Hi, Cari. I'm fine. Yourself?' Mark smiled, folding his tall frame into the chair next to Claire. 'Hey!' he mumbled to her briefly.

'Pretty good. What are you doing here, anyway?'

'We figured that if you two can swan off and 'do lunch', then we can too!' Lee winked at Mark. 'I phoned the hotel to see if Mark was at a loose end, and hey presto, here we are!'

Claire looked from Lee to Mark. How come Lee knew where Mark was staying? She didn't; it hadn't even crossed her mind to ask him. Having toured all over the world, he must be used to living out of a suitcase. It suited his lifestyle, and the way he was. That was probably why he had been so willing to postpone the date of their wedding. Twice. He did not like to be tied down; he loved his freedom too much.

Claire frowned. That's why she hadn't asked him. She didn't need to know. He was only in her life because of

Gemma; that was all. There was no need to know where he was staying, how he was doing in general, or anything like that. But when she turned her attention back to the other people at the table, she found that all three of them were chatting like old friends about Mark's house in London, and their favourite places to visit.

Something fluttered in Claire's stomach. She was thinking back to her conversation with Jennifer. She was horrified to find that she had a definite streak of jealousy racing around inside, so fast and so strong that she was sure that she was turning green.

How could she possibly be jealous? She had spent seven years of her life getting over the betrayal of her love by the man she was supposed to marry. And she was doing just fine, thank you very much; she had her own home, a lovely daughter, a wonderful job, with no need for anyone, any man, in her life.

So why on earth was she feeling this

way? Like her stomach was hollow, such was the strength of emotion, the feeling of loss. All those years on her own, deprived of a marriage that she had wanted with all her heart. It had grown, unsuspected and undetected, the second she had set eyes on Mark with Jennifer in the nightclub, until the moment she had answered Mark's mobile, hearing Jennifer on the other end.

Claire sat back in her chair with a look of stunned disbelief on her face, shocked at the realisation she had just reached. She was still in love with Mark. Claire's gaze automatically flickered to Mark, as Cari spoke.

'Do you have any plans for your birthday, Claire?'

'Birthday?' Claire frowned, having forgotten it was that time of year already. Claire looked at Mark again, then back to Cari. 'I . . . I hadn't really thought about it. I don't think I'll be doing anything at all,' she stammered nervously. 'Uh, I'll be right back!'

Claire's chair scraped across the floor noisily and almost tumbled over in her hurry to leave. It was only after she had made her way through the lunchtime crowd to the safety of the toilets that she realised she had been holding her breath. Gasping, she shakily locked the cubicle door and perched on the toilet seat. Her heart was hammering fit to burst, it hurt to breathe, her head was suddenly pounding and to top it all, as Claire brushed a strand of hair from her eyes, she found tears.

'Oh, God!' she moaned quietly, and bent her head into her hands. 'Why is this happening to me?'

Less than a week ago, she'd been doing just fine, and now, all because of Mark Crofts, she was an emotional wreck. She'd loved him, lived for him, would have died for him — but thought she was over him. How could she have been so blind?

With a sigh, Claire lifted her head and rubbed her temples. She still loved him, even after everything that had happened. Why else had she let Gemma plaster her bedroom walls with posters of him? Why else had she bought every single thing he'd released, under the pretense of buying them for her daughter? So she could see his face, listen to his voice, imagine he was still touching her, kissing her.

She shook her head to stop the thoughts, but she knew it was no use. She had been kidding herself all these years. She might have hated Mark once, when, alone and scared, she'd travelled to Newcastle, pursued by memories. But when she'd held their child in her arms, she knew that she would never be able to hate him, not for anything in the world.

Claire's tears had stopped now, and she blew her nose, trying to clear her head. So she still loved him, so what? What could possibly come of it? Mark had been shocked to find that he was a father after all this time, and although he seemed to genuinely care for Gemma, that was as far as it went.

When he had kissed her the other day, it had seemed so real, had felt as if he really wanted her. But it was gone as soon as Gemma appeared, and Claire had felt left out in the cold. Was he getting back at her, for leaving and not telling him about his child? Was he that heartless these days, that he could switch his emotions on and off? Did he hate her that much?

Mark may have changed in many ways, but the way he was with Gemma could not be faked. He wasn't so selfish as to break a little girl's heart, even to get back at her mother.

'No plans, no wishes, no tears,' Claire said aloud, stepping out of the cubicle. 'He is Gemma's father, and she has a right to be happy.' She checked her face quickly as she passed the mirror, brushing away a small trail of mascara under her eye, and then stepped back out into the bar.

The three of them had their heads together in a huddle as Claire approached the table and she felt a sinking feeling in her stomach. They had to be talking about her.

'There you are, love!' Cari said brightly, as Claire sat down. 'Thought you'd locked yourself in the toilet again!'

Mark smiled. 'Again?'

Lee started to laugh. 'She was seven months pregnant at the time!'

There was laughter, but Claire could hardly raise the corners of her mouth to smile. Every part of her felt like lead. She looked at Mark out of the corner of her eye. She had been alone for so long, and had convinced herself that Mark meant nothing to her. But now, the emotions which had lain dormant had been woken, and Claire had an unusually selfish desire to take any chance of being near Mark. She wanted to fill the hole he had made in her heart, albeit temporarily, for he would soon be on his way back to London, to his career, and to Jennifer.

'Have you and Jennifer discussed having children yet? I'm sure Gemma would love to have a little brother or sister.' The words were out of Claire's mouth before she could stop them, stemming from a sudden urge to find out how involved the two of them were.

Mark almost choked on a mouthful of coffee when he heard the question, and looked at Claire in surprise. 'What?'

'I said . . . '

'I heard what you said.' He looked at her. 'As a matter of fact, we were only talking about children the other day. Jennifer adores them and I think that she'd like to have a child soon. She'd make a really good mother!' he said smoothly, directing a sweet smile at Claire.

Claire was dumbfounded. She had been so sure that Mark was going to say no, that Gemma was enough for him at the moment, that he and Jennifer were nothing serious. And, a little voice whispered at the back of her mind, that he was still in love with Claire, and wanted to give up everything and come and live with her and Gemma in their cottage.

Claire looked into Mark's eyes, trying to see if there was anything else, but all they seemed to be saying to her was, 'Don't play games with me. You won't win!' But she had nothing to lose — except her heart, and that was already cracked right down the middle.

Mark turned to look at Cari. 'Is that settled for Saturday then, Cari?'

Saturday's my birthday, Claire thought.

'Yes, that's fine. I'll pick Gemma up at noon and then you can come over to lunch on Sunday.'

Claire looked warily around the table and found Lee beaming at her broadly.

'What's going on?'

'I'm taking you out for the evening, and Lee and Cari are looking after Gemma.' Mark smiled, but it didn't quite reach his grey eyes.

'You can't!' Claire blurted, then met Cari's gaze. She had been set up. She and Mark had not been alone properly for over seven years. Now, he wanted to take her out for dinner?

'You don't want to go?' Mark's tone was even, and there was no encouragement in his face for her to say yes, please.

Claire leant towards him, her eyes narrowed and her voice only slightly above a hiss. 'I thought you were here for Gemma, not me.'

Mark felt a cold shiver run down his back at the darkness of her eyes, and realised that it was excitement. He leaned in too, and reached under the table to squeeze her knee gently, making her jump in her seat. 'What's the matter — don't you want to be alone with me, Mitch?'

At that softly spoken challenge, and the nickname he used to use, combined with the touch of his fingers on her leg, Claire felt a ball of heat start low in her belly, sending little rivers of fire outwards. She met his gaze and was surprised to see an answering hunger there.

Suddenly embarrassed, Claire blushed.

'I should get back to the office. Cari, I had a great time, thanks. See you later, Lee!' She stood and picked up her belongings, stopping only to kiss Cari and Lee goodbye. Hoping she could get away without even having to look at Mark, she smiled broadly, if vaguely, around the table, and with a breezy ''Bye!' she headed for the door, heart hammering, breath uneven.

Claire was almost at the door, and told herself that she would calm down once she was outside in the fresh air. Then she felt someone behind her, felt a hand on her lower back. She looked over her shoulder. Mark had his coat on and seemed intent on leaving with her.

'What are you doing?' she asked, as he opened the door for her and guided her outside — probably a good thing, as she was not looking where she was going, her eyes solely on Mark.

'I'm taking you back to work. You got a taxi here, didn't you?' Claire nodded mutely. 'I thought I'd save you the walk.

If that's okay with you?'

Not waiting for an answer, Mark took her hand and led her to his Range Rover, which was parked back at the hotel, a five minute walk from the bar. As they came to a halt, Mark reached into his coat pocket for the keys, unlocked and opened the passenger door. 'After you!'

They were both silent as Mark negotiated the one-way system that had given him so much grief the day after he had met Claire again. It wasn't until they were more or less at their destination that Claire looked at him.

'What?' he asked, noticing her perusal of his face out of the corner of his eye.

Claire's mind scrambled for something to say, feeling guilty for being caught looking at him. 'I was just wondering what made you want to choose Scotland for a holiday. I thought you might prefer somewhere hot,' she added, remembering his golden tan in the middle of November.

'Doctor told me to rest. I chose

somewhere quiet.'

'Too many guest appearances at star-studded bashes with free booze? Or is it one too many late nights with Jennifer?' Claire intended it as a joke, but Mark did not see the humour. She saw a frown deepen on his face and he braked sharply outside of Stars, making her body jerk against the seat belt.

'That's not all I do, you know!' He undid his seat belt and halfway climbed into Claire's seat, his face a mere half foot away from hers.

'You could have hurt me! I hope you don't do that with Gemma in the car.' Claire was trying to get out of her own seat belt, but Mark reached for the release catch and pulled the strap tighter, so that she was pinned back in her seat. 'What are you playing at?' she exclaimed, looking at him.

'I should ask you the same thing. I'd like to know what you're more interested in, my relationship with Gemma, or my relationship with Jennifer — because you've brought her up in conversation a hell of a lot today.'

'Gemma, of course!'

'Then why the sudden interest in Jennifer?'

'Because anything you do with her is bound to have an effect on Gemma, that's why.'

Mark looked at her carefully as he moved away.

'Are you sure that's all?'

Shaking her head, Claire climbed out of the Range Rover. 'Thanks for the lift,' she mumbled.

She looked up as Mark crossed round to stand on the pavement in front of her.

'Look, all that stuff I said before, about Jennifer and babies. I may have been stretching the truth a bit. A lot. Honestly, we're really not that involved. It's more of a publicity thing. I'm sorry,' he said, genuinely.

Claire took it in, and realised she felt relief.

'Hey, aren't you going to ask me in for a coffee?' Mark grinned like a schoolboy and Claire couldn't help but smile.

'What are you on about, Mark?' The smile she gave him took him back to the days when they were together.

'When I used to drive you home in London, you'd always invite me in for a coffee,' he winked at her, 'or something else!'

'Mark!' Claire laughed, making him grin.

'Go on, Mitch!' Mark stepped closer towards her and, almost shyly, reached for her hand. 'It'll be just like old times.'

Claire looked deep into his grey eyes, in which she had once been able to see his soul, and saw a flicker of warmth. Encouraged and buoyed by that warmth, she moved closer to him. Standing on her tiptoes, she pressed her mouth to his.

'Seeing as you're here,' she whispered against his warm, soft lips, 'you might as well come in.' Then, running her fingers along his stomach, feeling his muscles tensing, she turned and walked up the steps towards the club.

As she punched in her code on the security panel, she could feel the heat radiating from him as he stood behind her. Leaning closer, he buried his face in her hair, and she could feel the warmth of his breath on her neck as he inhaled the scent of her. Her neck was very sensitive and with a smile, she bent her head into his, trying to alleviate the tickle of his breath, and an answering heat flamed through her veins.

Dear God, what was he doing? What was she letting him do? What had happened to the responsible single mother, who had always put her daughter's needs before her own? Why was she willing to let him touch her, kiss her, love her?

Love! Shaking her head, Claire stopped halfway through the open door, Mark bumping into her, thinking that she had stopped on purpose. His hands closed on her hips, creeping round the curves to rest lightly on her stomach.

Claire tensed, and tried to steel herself against her body's reaction to his touch. But it was no good. As much as her mind screamed stop, the beat of her heart, the rhythm of the coursing blood in her veins, the burning sensation where his hands rested on her body, urged her to carry on.

'Come on,' Mark whispered, gently pushing her through the door, and when Claire heard the slam of metal on metal, she knew there would be no turning back, not now, not ever. Her heart was his for the taking, like it always had been, always would be.

Claire remembered nothing of the steps she took to her office, conscious only of Mark's hand in hers. It was only when he shut her office door behind them that she remembered to breathe. As he turned the key, she felt the doors of her heart shut, locking Mark inside, where he should have been for the last seven years.

'Coffee?' Claire managed to say, looking at Mark as he approached her.

'Or something else?' he suggested, reaching for her, pulling her into the warm circle of his arms.

'Tea?' she tried weakly, seeing him smile.

'Kiss?' he countered, lowering his lips to hers.

The kiss that followed sealed Claire's fate. It was the way it should have always been, had she not run away all those years ago. As his lips tested hers, she tested her heart. It didn't seem to be hurting, like she had imagined it would if she let him close. In fact, it was beating fit to burst. Her hands reached for his shoulders, as much to brace herself as to pull herself closer to his warmth.

Mark followed her lead and wrapped his arms around her slim waist.

'Claire!' he muttered, taking his lips from hers for a split second.

She heard her name, heard Mark's voice, but couldn't respond even if she had wanted to. Every part of her, from mind to muscle, from skin to senses, was busy concentrating to the feel of his hands on her, the touch of his lips, the sweet taste of his mouth; she only managed to remember to breathe when Mark broke the kiss, loosening his grip on her, causing a sinking sensation in her stomach, a feeling of loss on her lips, and a sudden aching chasm in her heart.

'What is it?' she asked breathlessly, the stark look on his face beginning to raise questions in her hazed mind.

'Let's sit down.' Mark motioned towards the deep blue sofa, piled high with soft cushions.

He's going to tell me that he wants to take Gemma! A look of sheer panic crossed her face that second and Mark smiled.

'I want us to be comfortable, that's all. You look for all the world like a little girl who thinks I'm going to take her sweets away.'

Claire bit down on her lower lip. She did not seem to be able to meet his gaze, and Mark was reminded instantly of Gemma. God, they were so similar.

'Come on.' Mark took her hand.

After Mark had all but positioned her against the cushions, he tilted her head and she had to look at him. And what she saw took her breath away.

Mark's eyes were warm, caring and loving, taking her back to the days when she felt safe and wanted. Flames of passion roared in her belly and she wondered why she had ever left him. In a movement, Claire was wrapping her warmth around him, wanting him, needing him, loving him without words.

Dear God, had it been like this before? But the thought was soon chased away by fresh waves of longing; tremendous waves of want that started deep inside her, from her very core.

'Oh, Mark!' she finally gasped, but his muted reply was washed away by the shrill ringing of his mobile phone.

'Christ!' Mark moaned against her lips, tearing his hand away from her, intending only to delve into his pocket to toss the wretched piece of technology across the room, so that he could concentrate completely on this beautiful woman.

Claire felt his hand move quickly from its position, and felt as if she had suddenly been shoved out into the freezing night air, after being so deliciously warm by a great, roaring fire, and she pushed away from him abruptly.

'Phone, Mark!' she said curtly, refusing to meet his confused, enquiring gaze.

The phone's ring seemed to grow louder and more persistent the longer it went unanswered, echoing the ringing in Claire's own mind. 'Answer it, for God's sake!' she snapped, and hurled herself out of the sofa, and behind her desk, glaring at him as he reached into the pocket of his jacket and did as she bade him.

'What?' Mark barked, eyeing Claire as she paced up and down behind the huge desk that acted as a wall. 'What the bloody hell do you want, Justin? I thought I told you to leave me alone!'

'Nice to hear your voice too, Mark! This holiday of yours doesn't seem to be having quite the relaxing effect you'd hoped.' Justin's silken voice came down the line.

'What would you know?' Mark's question was automatic, but he knew that these last few days weren't exactly what his doctor would have prescribed for him either. Claire had seemed so eager to kiss him just seconds before, and now the temperature in the room had dropped dramatically from that of a scorching summer's day to what could only be described as sub-zero conditions. She was alternately shuffling papers on her desk and staring into space, her eyes glazing over.

'I know that every time I've spoken to you since you've been up there, you haven't been in the pleasantest of moods. Must be the company you're keeping.'

Mark caught Claire looking at him then with intense distrust, and he shifted in his seat nervously, even though he had no reason to. 'Look, whatever it is, can't it wait until I get back to London, Justin?'

'And when exactly will that be, Mark? You seem to be very vague at the moment and I don't have to remind you that you have responsibilities here!'

What was it with everyone trying to make him feel guilty all of a sudden? 'I have responsibilities here, too!' Mark snapped.

Claire's gaze homed in on him with missile-like accuracy, and a warning look flashed in her eyes. What the hell was he trying to do, drop hints that he had a six-year-old daughter running around in Newcastle? And to his slime ball of a manager as well!

'And do these, ahem, responsibilities involve millions of pounds, Mark? Will they make you happy when you look at your bank statement each month and see a row of noughts a mile long?'

'Screw you and your money, Justin! Is that all you ever think about? There's more to life than damn money!' Mark's frustration burst down the phone line and Justin began to think that he had just said the wrong thing. 'Don't phone me again, do you hear me?'

'I just wanted to know when you're coming home, that's all!' Justin changed tack. 'I need to arrange some dates, but I can't do that if you won't help me. I'm only trying to look after you.'

'You're my manager, Justin, not my wife. I don't need looking after. If I needed looking after, I would find myself a wife, settle down and have kids. You can't provide me with any of those, so get lost!'

With an angry jab of his forefinger, Mark terminated the conversation and flung the phone into the corner of the sofa, where it bounced off a cushion, and came to rest perilously close to the edge.

'Son of a . . . ' Mark muttered and then paused, finding Claire's eyes on him again, the hostility gone, replaced by a strange, unnameable emotion.

'What?' he asked.

'Did you have to mention the bit about responsibilities? You don't think Justin might find that phrase just a bit strange?' Claire's voice was quiet and level.

'Justin never listens to anything but the sound of his own voice. Anyway, I have got responsibilities. You and Gemma.'

'Don't drag me into it!' Her voice was high, as was her colour now. 'Don't go making any assumptions, Mark. I've already told you once that I'm not part of any deal!'

'I . . . ' All he could do was gape at her, not understanding how such a pleasant afternoon could turn into something resembling a studio meeting, with everyone fighting for, against and around him, but forgetting to let him in on the argument.

'I think you'd better go. No, on second thoughts, stay there. I'll go. I may not be able to walk out on you in my own home, but I can here!' Claire grabbed her bag and coat from the floor, unlocked the door and flounced out.

'You already did that, Claire, seven years ago,' Mark mumbled, as he put his face in his hands and sighed.

8

Claire got as far as the lobby in her dramatic exit and stopped in her tracks.

Responsibilities, Mark had said. Hadn't he just uttered the words she had never thought she would hear? Wasn't that what she wanted, deep down? He had told Justin that there was more to life than money. What else did she want from him?

'Going home already?' Lee's voice filtered into her thoughts and Claire looked up with a look of confusion on her face. 'What's happened? It's not Gemma again, is it?'

'Um . . . ' Claire looked at Lee, and her confusion cleared. 'No, I'm not going anywhere, and Gemma's fine. In fact, she'll be even better when Mark goes and picks her up from school. She'll be over the moon!' She smiled brilliantly at him, and turned back to her office. 'See you later.'

Lee stared, amazed — and not for the first time. Claire had always been on a constant level in all the years he had known her, but he never quite knew these days whether she was going to burst into tears or start laughing hysterically. Mark seemed to be having a major effect on her, whatever it was he was doing.

Mark was thinking much along the same lines when he heard the office door open and close again behind him. Turning his head to look over his shoulder, his gaze met Claire's.

'What now?' he asked, returning his head to its original position.

'I wondered if you wanted to go and pick Gemma up from school.' She took a seat next to him on the sofa, causing his phone to fall to the floor, unnoticed.

'Why? I mean, are you sure?'

Claire's grin was wide as she extracted pen and paper from her bag and hastily scribbled down directions out of the city to the school.

'Yes, I'm sure, and it would make her day. Pip's always one of the last ones out because she's too busy gassing with her friends. I'll let Cari and the school know that you're picking her up. Here.'

Mark was presented with the impromptu map, and again wondered at the sudden change in Claire. She seemed to be accusing him of all sorts of cruel and wicked things one moment and the next, she was willingly giving him access to the daughter she had deprived him of for so long. And try as he might to be angry with her, a smile on that beautiful face just for him was worth any kind of torture and pain as far as he was concerned.

'I'll bring her home straight away.'

'There's a spare key under the doormat. I'll be home later.'

'You're too trusting, Claire.' Mark kissed her gently on the lips as he stood up.

'Thanks.'

With a warm feeling welling up inside her, Claire watched him leave with a smile. It was so easy to love him, she decided — if she forgot what and who he was, and how many people had a part of him and his life. For now, she and Gemma were his responsibilities, he had said as much, and that made her smile anew. With a contented sigh, Claire stood and stretched, preparing herself for a couple of hours' work before she returned home to her daughter and Mark. Allowing herself to daydream, she pretended to finish her paperwork, a feeling of happiness bubbling inside her.

So engrossed was she in her fantasies of happy families, that an hour or so later, she did not hear the quiet ringing of a mobile. She hadn't even noticed that Mark's phone had fallen off the sofa when she had returned earlier, even less that she had gently kicked it under the piece of furniture. But ring it did, and the caller, getting no reply, decided to phone someone else.

* * *

Mark arrived at the school almost twenty minutes late and rushed into the building, panicking because there were very few cars outside in the car park, and he could not see anyone in the lobby and office.

'Hello?' he called, pulling open a door that led to the empty school hall.

Heading along a corridor, Mark repeated his greeting several times and then emerged into the open-plan classroom, where he found a woman and Gemma, who was quietly reading a book.

'Hi!' he said, somewhat breathlessly, and the woman and the little girl looked up at the same time.

'Daddy!' Gemma jumped out of her chair and into his arms in one movement. 'I thought Nana Cari had forgotten, or Mummy had an accident. No one told me you were coming.'

'Sorry, sweetheart.' Mark closed his eyes briefly as he hugged his daughter. 'We only just decided, and I got lost. Are you okay?'

'Mrs. Armstrong stayed with me.' Gemma gestured towards the woman who had now risen from her seat behind the desk and was discreetly trying to smooth her clothes.

'Hello Mr. Crofts, I'm Gemma's teacher, Mrs. Armstrong. I'm very pleased to meet you.' The woman extended her hand, and seemed reluctant to let go after Mark had politely accepted her greeting.

'Nice to meet you, and thank you for staying with Gemma. I'm sorry that no one was here to pick her up on time. It won't happen again.' Mark smiled at Pip, who was happily snuggled into his shoulder.

'It was my pleasure. Gemma is a lovely girl, and very bright too. If you would like to discuss her progress after school at any time, I would be more than happy to arrange a meeting with you.'

'Thanks, but I'm sure Claire can fill me in there. Besides, I'm only up here to see Gemma for a while before I have to head back to London.'

Gemma's little face fell at that last comment, but Mark didn't notice. Neither did he notice the sudden crafty expression on Mrs. Armstrong's face.

'Well, I'd better get Gemma home. Thanks again.' Mark smiled, and took Gemma and her belongings out to the car.

Having settled Gemma in the Range Rover, Mark climbed into the driver's side and shut the door. Gemma was very quiet, despite her initial enthusiasm at seeing him, and Mark looked at her.

'What's up, petal?'

'You said you were going back to London. When?' Gemma turned sad eyes to her father. 'I don't want you to go away. I only just got you.'

'Honey, I have to go back for work.'

'Why? Why can't you stay here with me and mum? You can work at Stars for Grandpa Lee, like Mum.'

'Pip . . . ' Words failed him and he didn't know what to do. Tears were beginning to form in the corner of the little girl's eyes. 'We'll have to sort something out with Mummy, eh? You can come and visit, and I can always come up here and see you. We'll have a talk, okay?' He reached out a gentle hand and stroked her hair.

'Can we phone her now?' Gemma brightened a little, and Mark smiled, reaching into his coat pocket.

The mobile wasn't there, and it wasn't in the other one either. 'Damn!' Mark muttered, causing Pip to look at him. 'Mum's got the phone. I left it in her office. We'll go home and call her from there.'

As Mark started the engine, Mrs. Armstrong watched the vehicle leave the school car park from a window in the staff room. Her fingers played with the edge of a newspaper that was open at the gossip pages on her lap. The woman's eyes scanned the print for the section she wanted, and picking up the phone on the table next to her, she dialled the London phone number.

'Hello, Top Pop Pages,' a male voice answered.

'Good afternoon. I was wondering if you would be able to help me?'

'What with?' The man at the other end was in a hurry, and shouldn't even have answered the phone. He'd been on his way to a staff meeting and was passing the phone as it started ringing. All of his reporters were already in his large office, he could see them through the glass walls. Someone had obviously forgotten to divert their phone to the answering machine. He had neither the time nor the patience to take the calls he had once been desperate for in his own days as a gossip gatherer for this daily paper.

'I read in your pages that you might be interested in some information I have, about someone famous. And that there may be some payment if you are interested in what I have to say?' The woman's voice rose hopefully at the end of her sentence.

'Okay, love. Who is it you've slept with then?'

'I beg your pardon! I happen to be happily married. Which is more than I can say for Mark Crofts!'

One of the staff reporters stuck his head round the door to see if his boss wanted him to take over the call, but when Graham Short heard that name, he waved him away and rounded the desk to sit down.

'My name is Graham Short. And you are . . . ?'

'Mrs. Armstrong.'

'Okay, Mrs. Armstrong. Would you like to tell me exactly what it is you know about Mark Crofts?'

As the woman started to describe the situation with Claire and Gemma, and her own consequent meeting with Mark not half an hour before, Graham was making notes on a piece of paper.

'And you say that Mark is in Newcastle as we speak?' he asked.

'Yes. In fact, he was right here until just before I called you. Mr. Smith, when will I receive my, er, fee for this information?'

Graham rolled his eyes heavenward, but told her politely, 'I'm afraid I will have to check out a few facts before I can ascertain any form of payment, Mrs. Armstrong. Let me pass you onto one of my colleagues who can take your details and we will get back to you as soon as we can. Just a moment!'

Graham stabbed the hold button with his finger and motioned for someone to come over.

'Get rid of her, whatever it takes!' he said over his shoulder to the junior staff member as he headed for his office. Sticking his head through the door, he said, 'Right, I'm afraid I have to postpone the meeting until another time, guys. Something has come up that needs my attention immediately. I'll let you know when I can rearrange. Thanks!' He dismissed everyone, amid much mumbling.

As soon as the last person had shut the door behind them, Graham picked up his phone. Dialling the number, he waited until the answering service clicked on.

'Where are you, Mark? Call me.' Graham replaced the receiver and stared at the phone.

Graham and Mark had met four years before, just as Mark had left the band, at a time when Graham was working hard to secure his position as editor of the popular Top Pop Pages in the Informer daily newspaper. Graham had grabbed the scoop interview with Mark, and since then, they had been firm friends. If this information was true, he could not believe that Mark had never told him.

According to this Armstrong woman, Mark was in Newcastle playing happy families with a woman called Claire Montague and their six-year-old daughter, Gemma. Allegedly, Mark hadn't been around for a long time, and now had put in an appearance. Christ, the press would have a field day with this one!

Mark had provided Graham with a lot of scoops over the years, and Graham had protected his friend's privacy as far as he could in the unscrupulous world of the press. However, Graham's protection could only do so much.

Of late, Mark had been in the gossip pages of magazines and newspapers daily, and it had distressed him so much that he was now taking a holiday to get away from it all. He'd try Justin. If anyone knew how to get hold of Mark, he would. Graham found his number and dialled. At the very least, he could try and get warning to Mark before Mrs. Armstrong took her gossip elsewhere . . .

* * *

'Lee, I have a call for you. Justin Lloyd-Smith,' Rachel informed Lee as he was preparing to leave for the evening. Claire had already gone, happy to be heading home to Mark and

Gemma, who had called to say they had made dinner for her.

'Put him through, Rachel, and then you might as well go home. I'll see you tomorrow.' Taking off his coat again, Lee prepared to sit down. Justin could talk for hours. 'Justin, what can I do for you?'

'I won't keep you long, Lee. I know you're a busy man.' Justin sounded worried about something, and Lee raised a silent eyebrow. 'I just wondered if you'd seen Mark at all since last week?'

'Why?'

'Something urgent has come up and I really need to talk to him.'

'Isn't he supposed to be on holiday?' Lee wasn't sure where this was leading.

'True, but this could affect the rest of his career. Now, I ask you, is that not urgent enough to talk to him for a few minutes, whether he is on holiday or not?' Justin paused for effect, knowing Lee was a soft touch for a sob story. 'Have you seen him?'

'Yes, I have.'

'Where is he, then?' Justin's façade slipped slightly, although Lee simply took it as concern for Mark.

'He's here in Newcastle still.'

'Can you reach him for me? Do you have a number? I really need to speak to him, Lee. You wouldn't hold out on an old friend, after everything we've done for each other?'

Lee paused, deciding that Justin was up to his usual tricks again.

'Tell you what I'll do, old *friend*, I'll ask Mark to call you next time I see him. How's that?'

'It's not good enough! You have to tell me!' Justin screeched down the phone.

'Nice talking to you, Justin. I'll pass the message on. Take care now!' Lee ended the conversation, and marvelled at Justin's nerve. Mark was on holiday, and Justin still wanted to have complete control of his life. Well, this was one message that Lee would not be passing on. In fact, he would forget that Justin had called at all.

With a smile, Lee donned his coat, switched off the light and closed the office door on the shrill ringing of the telephone. Saying goodnight to various members of his staff on the way out, Lee stepped out into the cold November air. He was looking forward to a quiet night in with his lovely wife for once, forgetting all about his nightclub, and his other ventures, knowing that all of his staff were loyal, and had the same goals as he had when it came to the success and smooth running of his business.

Yes, he could be quite content, and proud, of his achievements. On the drive home, he toyed again with the idea of letting Claire take over the running of Stars, and maybe a couple of the other concerns he had in the northeast. She had more than proved herself over the last seven years, and she enjoyed the work as much as Lee had always done.

With an even wider smile, Lee kissed

his wife as she opened the front door to him. For her part, Cari was very pleased to see him so much earlier than expected. And over dinner, her satisfaction grew at having him happy to be there instead of worrying what was happening at Stars, as he talked over his idea of surrendering the majority of control to Claire.

Claire, meanwhile, was at her own dinner table, eating a meal with her daughter and the man she loved. Her smile shone in her eyes and Mark spent the majority of the meal bathing in the happiness that he saw there, hoping that he had something to do with her current joy.

Claire was indeed happy. This was how she had always envisaged her life when she was a little girl: sitting around the table with her dad, her mum and her sister, before the dreaded familiarity of the press had struck. If she tried hard enough, she could remember her own mother doing the same things for her that she now did for Gemma, and for a moment, the memory made her heart constrict and tears spring to her eyes. Perhaps she should get in contact with her family again. After all, look how easily things were going with Gemma and Mark, how simply things had slotted together. Would Gemma not love to have a famous aunt and grandmother?

If things had been different between her and Mark, if they had stayed together and brought Gemma up together, wouldn't it have been a natural process to let her mother and her sister back into her heart?

Claire took a gulp of air to stop the unshed tears in her eyes, for it would only worry Gemma and cause Mark to think there was a problem, when in fact she was the happiest she had been in years — as long as she didn't allow herself to think further than the end of Mark's vacation.

Looking at Gemma, Claire knew that it would crucify her if anything ever caused a split between them. That was why she had been so concerned about the effect Mark was going to have on their daughter. It hadn't occurred to Claire until now that her own mother might have had much the same feeling at Claire's sudden and unannounced departure, shortly after her father's death. Had her mother felt the hurt and pain and loss that Claire knew she would have felt if Mark ever decided to try and take Gemma away? This sudden thought caused a rush of guilt to flood her already rosy cheeks, as she considered the pain she must have caused her mother, albeit not deliberately, suffering another unimaginable loss so close on the heels of her husband's death.

Claire's eyes met Mark's then, but she could not hold his gaze. How could she accuse Mark of being selfish after all these years, when she herself had deprived him of his daughter, much the same as she had deprived her mother of a grandchild and her sister of a niece? A tear escaped from her lowered lashes and Mark felt stricken as he watched the tear glide, unhindered by the brush of a hand, down her flushed cheek.

'Finished, Pip?' Mark glanced at the child, noting that she had eaten everything on her plate, her knife and fork placed neatly together. He smiled fleetingly at the little girl's lovely manners, showing to the world how well Claire had brought her up thus far. 'Why don't you go and get ready for bed, darling?'

Gemma's face fell, as she thought she was being sent to bed, and it wasn't even her bedtime. 'I haven't had my pudding yet!' she protested, thinking of the lovely chocolate pudding they had made from the packet.

'If you go up now, I'll bring it up to you in bed,' Mark bargained, noting that another tear was following the same path as its predecessor.

'But I'm not allowed to eat in bed. Mum says . . . '

'I'm sure Mum won't mind this one time. Now, go on!' Mark interrupted her and nodded his head toward the kitchen door. He waited until the pouting child had said thank you for a lovely dinner and had left the room, before he scooted across into Gemma's vacated chair, at right angles with Claire.

'Why are you crying, Mitch?' His hand sought hers across the table.

At his touch, she looked up through shining tears. 'I'm sorry, Mark. I've been so selfish.'

'Hush, now! What are you talking about?' His voice was soothing, as he stroked her hand. 'How have you been selfish?'

'I've kept Gemma to myself all this time.' Mark started to quieten her with denials, but Claire needed to finish. 'No, listen. When you came back, all I could think about was losing her, of spending the rest of my life without her, when she is my whole world. I would rather die than live without her. And yet, I put my mother through exactly the same thing!'

'Claire, your mother loves you. If you

were to call her right now, she would be the happiest person on this earth. She would give anything to see you, anything.' Mark's hands squeezed her shoulders tightly, trying to reassure her, to stop her tears from falling.

'You don't understand, Mark!' She raised her eyes to his.

'Yes, I do. More than you think. I've seen your mum, and Rebekah, a few times since you left.'

'What?' Her eyes widened as she tried to take in what he'd said.

'It's only been professionally, at parties or presentations or whatever. They miss you, Claire, very much.'

Claire was shaking her head now.

'Listen to me. I know you never expected to meet up with me again, and I know I gave up hope years ago of ever seeing you. But just because you're not in someone's life anymore, it doesn't mean that they forget you, and your mother's no different. She wants to see you, and I know she'd be over the moon about Gemma.'

His urging words and eager expression caused Claire's heart to start hammering, her breath to come quick and shallow. His firm grip on her shoulders felt like a vice all of a sudden, and she could feel the walls closing in on her again

Reconciliation with her mother and sister would bring with it unbearable press attention. It would be the hottest story in Katherine and Rebekah Mitchell's lives since the death of Luke Mitchell ten years ago. The number one bestsellers and millions of magazine covers worldwide would mean nothing compared with an emotional reunion of mother, sister, daughter and granddaughter, torn apart by tragedy and brought together again by the most sought-after man of the decade.

Claire's throat constricted as she imagined the circus that would engulf them all. She took a breath.

'Gemma will be waiting for her pudding. You should take it up to her before she feels neglected!' Claire managed to smile, even though she was going to pieces inside.

Mark took his hands away from her shoulders and contemplated her in silence for a moment. 'I doubt she has ever felt neglected,' he noted warmly, and stood up.

Claire tried to concentrate on his movements around the kitchen as he took the chocolate mousse from the fridge and set about dishing it up into three bowls, but her eyes were swimming and her head was pounding. All she could think about was the last time she had seen her mother and her sister, and it left a sour taste in her mouth.

Mark had made every effort for her eighteenth birthday; all of her friends in London had been invited to a party in a restaurant in Soho that she and Mark often visited, and it had all been a complete surprise. Claire remembered feeling overwhelmed at the trouble he had gone to, and it had brought tears to her eyes that her father was not there to help her celebrate or to see how proud she was of Mark and how much she loved him. There were many presents, gifts from all her friends, but Mark had kept one gift secret from her and she was dying to know what it was.

A secret part of her was hoping that it was an engagement ring, showing that he wanted to spend the rest of his life with her, loving only her. In her wildest dreams, she had never imagined that he would present her mother and sister to her, complete with armfuls of presents and accompanied, as always, by the mob of photographers and reporters who followed their every move.

As her mother had swept across the crowded restaurant, her arms open wide, her eyes full of tears, her face filled with hope, Claire felt a rush of love for the woman she had not seen in two years, whom she missed more than she could say, and stepped towards her. But then the photographers, seeing a front page in the next day's tabloids, started snapping pictures, the flashes bright and blinding, and Claire was instantly transported back to the day of her father's funeral. It was too much pain and heartache to face again and she turned her back on her mother and sister and fled to the toilets.

Unaware of the turmoil she had created in the restaurant, Claire had slumped against the locked door of a cubicle and laid her head on her knees, silent tears falling. It wasn't until much later, when she and Mark had taken a taxi to her rented flat, that she spoke, and then it was in a quiet voice, taut with pain.

'Why did you do it, Mark?' she had asked, looking out of the cab window.

'Why did I do what?' Mark's voice had trembled with barely controlled anger. 'I should be asking you that question. What the bloody hell did you think you were playing at? Do you know how much trouble I went to, to get them both to come? Do you?'

Claire had flinched and moved closer

to the door of the cab. 'You don't understand!'

'You're damn right I don't understand, Claire! How could you treat your own mother like that? Completely ignoring her when she'd made the effort to reschedule her engagements to be at your party?'

'She shouldn't have to make an effort! If I meant that much to her, she should have dropped everything to be with me, like she should have done when my father died. But no, she was far too wrapped up in her own grief and how she would look in the papers to worry about me!' Claire's voice had broken as the tears started to flow down her flushed face.

'Claire, I . . . '

'Don't Claire me! You don't know. You weren't there. She insisted all the photographers came into the churchyard where we were burying my dad. I had to walk behind his coffin, trying not to cry, with all these lights flashing in my face, and voices shouting at us to look at them so that they could get a good picture. My father was the most important person in my life and I couldn't even say goodbye to him in peace, with all these people wanting to be part of the show my mother had created.'

Claire had stopped to take a deep breath, to calm herself down. 'I lost the rest of my family that day, along with my father. The only thing that could have kept us together that day was my mother. I was fifteen, Mark, I didn't know how to cope with that loss. And yet, the first time in years that I actually wanted something from my mother, she failed. I wanted her to respect my father's privacy in his last moments, especially after the press had crawled all over the car wreck before the ambulance even got there. But no, she insisted on having them there, to catch every glorious moment.'

'I'm sure she only wanted to give your father the tribute he deserved, Claire!'

'What my father deserved?' Claire had snorted in disgust. 'My father was a quiet man, he didn't like the attention any more than I did, but because he loved my mother, he put up with it. I know damn well that he would never have wanted the side-show that his funeral turned into!'

'I'm sorry. I never knew it was like that.'

'And I hope you never will, Mark. I hope that you never, ever have to go through what I did. I honestly hope that you never feel that much loss in your life, because until you do, you will never understand how I feel. Never!'

Then the taxi had pulled to a stop outside Claire's home. Mark had moved to come in with her but Claire shook her head and closed the taxi door behind her. And with the closing of the car door, had come the first barricade around her heart.

Now, Claire shook her head to clear the memory, but she could still see the camera bulbs flashing in her mind's eye. With the lights came a blinding headache and she staggered to her feet, intent on making it to the safety of her bedroom, to the darkness, where she could hide and try to forget the pain of the past and the pain that she knew was yet to come. She couldn't take any more; she had no strength left to fight the consequences of her own actions. Her eyes were swimming as she left the kitchen, and she could not see clearly to make her way to the stairs.

Mark was just in time to catch her as she fainted in the hallway, dropping Gemma's empty dessert bowl in his haste to save her from hitting the solid wooden floor. Carrying her into the living room, he deposited her gently on the sofa, talking to her softly, making her comfortable against the cushions, smoothing her hair from her damp brow.

Claire's eyes fluttered open and then closed against the bright light of the lamp, and Mark reached for the dimmer switch on the wall behind the sofa. Tears lined her eyelashes as she tried to open her eyes once more, grateful for the darkness.

'What happened?' she muttered, trying to sit up, but her head was pounding too hard for her to concentrate on anything.

'You fainted. How are you feeling?'

'Tired. Where's Pip?'

'In bed, nearly asleep. I wish I could fall asleep that easily.' Mark knew he was talking nonsense but he couldn't deal with seeing Claire like this. She had always been the strong one in their relationship, even if she hadn't known it.

She had shared her strength with him when she had held him close, she had given him confidence when she smiled at him in that special way, and when they had made love, she made him complete, ready to fight for everything he believed in and for everyone he loved.

The last time he had seen her lying like this was when she was in hospital, after she had tripped and fallen down the stairs at their flat. She had been so still and quiet, as if the spark had left her body, and it had frightened him.

Looking at her now, her high colour and the unshed tears still lingering on her closed lashes, he felt completely useless, as he had when she was in hospital. If he did not even know what to do when someone had fainted, how the hell would be have known what to do with a new-born baby had he and Claire stayed together for the birth? He didn't acknowledge the fact that he would have been prepared to a certain extent for the arrival of his daughter into this world had he been there during the run-up to her birth. All Mark knew was that he had stopped letting people get close to him after Claire's departure.

For Mark, at that moment in time, looking at Claire asleep on the sofa, all he could think of was the emptiness that flooded through him, leaving him feeling hollow. What good was all that adulation, all that fame and all that money, if he had no one to share it with? When he went home at night, he was greeted by a great big house filled with antiques and classic artwork, but in reality, it was a shell. Just like his heart.

Many minutes later, Mark's reverie was broken by the sound of his daughter's voice, crying plaintively in the night for her mother, and as he soothed the little girl to sleep, a sense of longing and of extreme loss washed over him.

9

Claire awoke the next morning with a strange sense of déjà-vu. The house was silent, it was late and she had a throbbing headache. With an effort, she swung her legs over the side of the bed and sat up. Her eyes swam a little, but after rubbing them with her fists, her vision cleared and she looked around. Her bedside clock told her it was after one o'clock in the afternoon, and looking down, she found she was dressed in only her underwear. She didn't remember going to bed, let alone getting undressed.

A blush came to her cheeks as she surmised that Mark must have put her to bed. She remembered vaguely that he had placed her gently on the sofa in the lounge, but that was it. Why did she feel so strange, almost embarrassed, that he had taken her clothes off, when he had seen it all before?

She spotted a piece of paper next to the clock. Unfolding it, she discovered it was a note from Mark. He had taken Gemma to school that morning, and had phoned Lee to let him know that she wouldn't be in work today. She was to phone Cari when she woke up, and Mark would pick Pip up from school and take her out for something to eat.

Claire raised an eyebrow at that point, wondering whether she had given Mark permission for an unaccompanied outing, especially when she was that paranoid about anyone spotting Mark with his daughter. But, in reality, Claire knew she could trust him, especially after his conversation with Justin the day before.

Justin! The events of yesterday, and the emotions that she had experienced, came flooding back full force; feelings for Mark, for her mother, her father and her sister, that had been locked inside her for years. Tears rolled down Claire's cheeks. She felt emotionally drained. With a sob, she flopped listlessly back onto the bed, and gave into her tears, eventually falling into an exhausted sleep. She didn't wake, even when a worried Cari let herself in, and tucked the duvet snugly around her, smoothing her hair back from her now peaceful face.

Several phone calls later, from Mark checking with Cari on how Claire was, and to tell her that he and Gemma were going into town to go to a games arcade, Claire finally woke, much rested and feeling a whole lot better after a long shower.

Cari made her an omelette, not sure how big her appetite would be, but Claire polished it off with speed, then devoured a huge sandwich and a plate of chips.

'You were hungry!' Cari laughed as Claire sat back with a contented smile on her face. 'I haven't seen you eat that much since you were pregnant with Gemma!'

'I guess I was really empty,' Claire

said, and when Cari frowned, not comprehending what she meant, she explained.

'I was a mess last night, Cari. Mark mentioned that he had seen Mother and Rebekah. I confronted a lot of feelings that I had never let myself think about. I cried a lot, and now I feel . . . I don't know, lighter, somehow. Does that sound weird?' Claire looked at the older woman with a puzzled expression, then shook her own head.

Cari did not pursue it and filled Claire in on Mark and Gemma's activities for the afternoon.

'It's funny,' Claire mused, over a cup of coffee.

'What is?' Cari asked.

'If you'd have asked me ten days ago, even a week ago, if I'd have let Mark take Gemma somewhere by himself, I'd have laughed at you, or called him every name under the sun. I never imagined letting myself agree to it.'

'Ten days ago, I didn't even know that you knew Mark, let alone that he

278

was the father of your child!'

'I didn't know that I would feel like this. It's all happened so quickly, Cari.' Claire smiled at her friend, and then looked at her questioningly. 'Didn't you ever wonder who Gemma's father was? You and Lee never asked me anything about it.'

'Of course we wondered, love. But it was obvious that it wasn't something you wanted to talk about.'

'It was a fresh start for me when I came up here. I'm really grateful, you know, for everything you and Lee have done for me and Gemma. I don't think we'd have ever coped on our own.'

Cari reached across the table and patted Claire's hand in a gesture of affection. 'Yes, you would. You're a very strong young woman, Claire. It might have been difficult for a while, but you'd have sorted yourself out.'

'Well,' Claire drained her cup and stood up, planting a kiss on the woman's cheek, 'I'm glad I didn't have to!'

Cari smiled as she watched Claire rinse the cup in the sink. Claire turned and leant against the counter.

'Am I doing the right thing, Cari? I mean, letting Gemma get used to Mark being her father, letting her get close to him? Am I setting her up for a big fall?'

'Is that what you think?'

'I don't know, to be honest.' Claire pulled her hair back from her face with both hands, holding the glowing curls at the back of her head. 'I'm confused. One minute, I think it's all okay, I can handle it. It's almost as if Mark has been around since the beginning. He's so natural with her and she adores him. But then . . . ' Claire's voice trailed off as she stared into space, lost in her own thoughts.

'What about how you feel about Mark?' Cari asked quietly.

'I just told you!' Claire looked at her.

'No, you told me how you felt about Mark and Gemma. Not what's been happening between you and Mark. You forget, Claire. I know you, I know what you've been through the last six years. I was there when you gave birth. You've always shared your thoughts and problems with me, but now, it seems like you've gone back into yourself, like you were when you first arrived.'

Claire looked surprised. 'I didn't realise.'

'You've spent so much time worrying about Gemma and how this is all going to affect her. What about how it's affecting you? Have you thought about that?'

'Too much!' Claire exclaimed. 'Sorry, but I've spent so much time struggling with this. I've come to the conclusion that if it all goes wrong, Gemma is young enough to get over it. It'll hurt for a while, but she will always have this time with Mark to remember. At least it's not a secret anymore, that's one less strain I have to cope with.'

'And will you be able to cope? Can you cope, if he leaves?'

'I'll manage. He didn't really have a choice when I left him. He didn't know about the baby. But, if he decides to leave, then it will be his choice. He knows her now, and he will have to choose.'

'So things haven't . . . ' Cari stopped, causing Claire to prompt her to go on. 'What I mean is, has anything happened between you two?'

'Not really.' The blush which appeared on Claire's cheeks caused Cari to smile. 'Okay, okay!' Claire grinned. 'We've kissed.'

'And?'

'And? Cari, I can't believe you're asking me this!' Claire laughed.

'Come on, it's not every day a good-looking pop star turns up in your life!'

'He hasn't always been a pop star. Remember, I knew him before.'

'And how! There's Gemma to prove that. You can't tell me he doesn't stir anything up in you. He does me!'

'Caroline Louise McGuire!' Claire exclaimed and the two women were laughing heartily when Gemma and Mark entered the kitchen.

'Mum!' Gemma ran to her mother, pleased to see her looking so happy. She had been worried when Claire hadn't woken her up for school that morning, but Mark had made it all seem like fun, and when he had tried to get her into her school uniform, he had made such a mess of it, Gemma was in a fit of giggles. 'Are you better?' Gemma turned her grey eyes, so much like her father's, to look lovingly at Claire, who smiled and kissed her upturned face.

'Yes, darling. I'm feeling a lot better, thank you. So, what have you and your dad been up to?' She looked over her daughter's head at Mark, who was laden with two teddy bears and various knick-knacks they had won at the arcade. He smiled at her and shrugged as best he could with a large stuffed toy under each arm.

'We went to the arcade, and then we had hot dogs and chips, with red sauce!' Gemma said, somewhat unnecessarily as Claire could see the remains of the meal on her white school shirt.

'Looks like you cleaned up!' Cari laughed, standing to relieve Mark of the booty. 'Why don't we go and get you a bath, Pip? I think your dad could do with a break.'

Gemma kissed her mum before grabbing a teddy bear and following Cari upstairs to the bathroom.

Mark pulled out a chair and sat down with a sigh.

'She's got a lot of energy!' he complained, as Claire laughed at him.

'She's six! Plus, you stuffed her with lots of calories and no doubt lots of sugar.' Claire looked at the empty sweet wrappers that Mark pulled out of his pocket and deposited on the table.

'Is she not allowed them?' Mark looked at her enquiringly.

Claire smiled, reaching for the wrappers. 'Would you like a cup of tea? You look worn out.'

'How about a glass of wine?' Mark asked hopefully.

'Sure.'

Mark watched her as she moved

around the kitchen.

'You look a lot better than you did last night.'

Claire turned to look at him as she put two wine glasses on the counter. 'Last night?'

'You sort of fainted. Don't you remember?'

'Not really. I remember talking about some stuff. Mum and Rebekah. Then I woke up this morning,' she looked him full in the eye, 'in my underwear.'

Mark's grin matched hers as she sat down. 'I didn't think you'd be comfortable fully dressed.'

'Hmm.' Claire smiled at him as she handed him a glass of wine,

'Are you feeling better, then? You had me quite worried for a while.'

'Why?' Claire was curious.

Mark contemplated his drink for a while.

'When you fainted, I put you on the sofa. You looked so much like you did when . . . '

Mark picked up his glass and took a

swig. 'The last time I saw you, Claire, you were in the hospital. You were lying in that bed and you looked so fragile. It was the same last night, except you didn't leave. I was there to put you to bed, I was there when you woke up last night, and I was there for you this morning, except you didn't know it.'

Claire could not meet his gaze, so intense was the expression on his face. She knew that he was heading towards something big and she wasn't sure that she was ready to hear it. So far, in their short re-acquaintance, all they had really talked about was Gemma. They had touched occasionally on their past life together, but from the look in Mark's eyes, she knew that they were getting down to the grass roots of their history together.

'Mark, I . . . '

'No, let me say this. If we never talk about this again, Claire, at least it will be out in the open.'

'I don't think this is the right time, Mark.'

He reached across for her hand. 'Claire!'

'Mark, please.' She looked him in the eye then and saw his pain. 'If you do this, you have to think of what it means for Gemma. She's the only one that matters.'

'It's not just about Gemma though, is it?' Mark pulled her to him. 'She's not the only one who matters. You matter. We matter. There are things we need to talk about. You've carried it all by yourself. I'm here now.'

Claire braced her hands on his shoulders, desperate to keep some distance between them. If he pulled her closer, if she felt his body against hers, there would be no hope for her heart.

'It's in the past. We were young. It didn't work out. It happens, Mark. We're just one of the millions of couples who have a child and split up.'

'Slightly different for us. You left me — and then you had our child. I don't believe I was involved in any of that.' Mark's voice sounded tight.

'Can't we just forget about it and move on?' Claire forced herself to speak in a bright tone, but it obviously didn't come out right. She could see his face darken. His eyebrows pulled down in a frown, his eyes narrowed and his lips thinned as he pressed them together.

'That's just it, I can't forget about it. I can't move on. I've not had a single, committed relationship since you, Claire, not one.'

'Perhaps you haven't found the right woman yet?'

'I did, but you bolted out of the door so fast your feet didn't touch the ground. For goodness' sake, just take some responsibility for it, will you? Stop dodging the facts. You left me, not the other way around. You decided, in your wisdom, to walk out of our life together. You didn't discuss it with me. You didn't give me a chance to explain. You left me with no idea as to where you had gone. No clues so I could come and find you. You gave up on us and our future.'

'I had my reasons.'

'I know, and I will forever be sorry for what you saw that day, for what I did. But why didn't you just speak to me? Claire, please, just tell me why.' He caught Claire's face between his hands. To make her look at him.

'You chose your career over our future!' Claire exclaimed.

'How? You were a part of everything I did. It was all done for you, for us.'

'Justin told you not to marry me.'

Mark frowned. 'It was a discussion we had, yes.'

'You had it in my hospital room. In front of me.'

'You were unconscious.'

'Clearly not! I'd come round, but when he turned up, I closed my eyes and waited for him to go. Justin said it would ruin your career if we got married. And you agreed with him, no hesitation.' Claire's throat tightened.

'Maybe you'd not come round as much as you think. I didn't agree with him, Claire. I wasn't about to call off our engagement on Justin's say-so.'

Claire shook her head, thinking of the dream she used to have so often when she was pregnant. Could she have got it wrong? But she carried on.

'I think you do whatever Justin asks you to.'

'What's that supposed to mean?'

They both could hear the thud of steps — Gemma, coming down the stairs.

'He can still pull your strings. He got you to attend opening night at Stars, didn't he?'

'That was a favour for Lee.'

'You didn't know Lee then,' Claire hissed, her mouth close to his ear so Gemma wouldn't hear. Gemma's voice came through the door, talking to Cari.

'You don't know me anymore, you can't make that assumption about me,' Mark whispered back, fiercely, his breath warm against her skin, lips brushing her ear.

'I clearly didn't know you then,

either,' she retaliated, turning her head to look at him.

'You know this!' Mark moved his hands to her face, sliding his fingers into her hair to bring his lips against hers. 'You know I want you!'

The door handle rattled but Claire couldn't seem to take her lips from his. Of the two of them, Mark reacted the quicker.

'I'll go!' He removed his body from hers and went out into the hallway, closing the door behind him. Claire kept her eyes fixed on the door, waiting for him to come back.

She heard Gemma run back up the stairs and slam her bedroom door and then she heard Cari call out goodbye and the front door close. She waited for Mark but he didn't come. I'll go, he'd said. Had he? Claire felt the panic welling up from the pit of her stomach. Had he really gone?

She dithered for a few more moments, moving aimlessly around, tidying things, before she plucked up the courage to open the door. Her common sense told her it didn't matter if he had left. It was what he would do eventually — return to his normal life. Better to get it over than prolong the inevitable.

He wasn't in the lounge or the study, or in the cupboard under the stairs. Claire headed upstairs and stuck her head round Gemma's door. The little girl was buried under the duvet, and the covers were quivering. He had gone, and Gemma was crying.

'Oh, sweetheart, it's okay,' Claire crooned, kneeling by the side of the bed, stroking the trembling body. The trembles strengthened to a definite shake. Claire frowned. Why wasn't Gemma making a sound? Her child never cried quietly. She made sure everyone knew it. Something else was going on.

A snigger escaped from under the bedding and Claire pulled back the duvet. Her daughter lay on her side, her small body convulsing with laughter, a teddy bear pressed to her mouth.

'What the . . . ?'

Gemma laughed out loud at the look of confusion on her mother's face. 'I told Daddy you were no good at hide and seek!'

'We're playing hide and seek?'

'Daddy's hiding too. You've got to find him next.'

Claire had to smile at Gemma's giggles. 'And Daddy says I have to go to sleep now. 'Night, Mum.'

Claire searched the bathroom and the spare bedroom. He was in neither. That only left her bedroom. She paused in the doorway and then slowly shut it behind her, plunging the room into near-total darkness. She reached for the light switch.

'Don't.' Mark's voice sounded so close to her in the dark room, but when she reached out she found only an empty space. 'You're cold.'

Claire wondered what he was playing at. She took a step forward.

'Still cold.'

Another step, then another. Her legs

touched the edge of her bed.

'Tepid.'

There weren't many places to hide in the room. Maybe he was on the bed? Claire launched herself onto the bed and came up with her pillow.

'Lukewarm!' Claire could hear the smile in his voice and got a better idea of where he was. The window on the side of the room had floor-length curtains. Claire inched her way across the floor.

'Warmer,' Mark said.

'Hot?' she asked, as Mark parted the curtains, the moon shining through the window behind him.

Mark smiled, and took her face gently in his hands, stroking the pad of his thumb across her parted lips.

'Definitely.'

Claire gave her mouth up to his, matching his passion, her own desire growing from deep inside. As Mark's lips trailed along the edge of her jaw, to her neck, Claire could feel the warmth of his breath. His fingers drew her hair back over her shoulder, stroking the sensitive skin, blazing a path of pleasure. The kisses that followed stoked the heat within her core.

Mark lowered her onto the bed and lay beside her, taking her in his arms, loving her in all the ways she'd missed every night since she had run away, until they fell asleep, together.

Claire woke the next morning with a smile on her lips.

'What are you grinning at?' That sexy voice was so close.

Claire opened her eyes and rolled onto her side. Mark was sitting on the edge of the bed and she curled her legs against his solid back under the duvet. It was out of long-forgotten habit and a desire to be connected to him.

Throughout the years, this was what she had missed the most, just being near him, being able to reach out, touch him, be held by him. The physical reassurance that she was not alone filled an ache in her heart and Mark seemed to sense it.

He pulled back the duvet. 'Move over.' He soon had the entire length of his body against hers, wrapping her in his arms, entangling his legs with hers.

'I've missed this. I've missed you.'

Claire smiled against his lips, pressing her mouth to his, urging him to hold her tighter, squeezing him to tell him she'd missed this too, cupping his face as she kissed him deeply.

'Careful, Claire, our daughter's only next door,' Mark warned.

'Is she awake?'

'She wasn't earlier.' His breath was warm against her as he traced a line to her collarbone.

'Mum, I've got the papers!' a sing-song voice called, followed by the thump of her daughter pounding up the stairs.

'The papers?' Mark asked.

'We always read them in bed together on a Saturday. She likes the cartoons,' Claire said, grimacing, as she rolled out of the bed to grab her dressing gown, pulling the duvet to cover Mark with a second to spare.

Gemma burst into the room, all of a flurry, and then stopped, her mouth a perfectly round O.

'Morning, Gem,' Mark smiled at his daughter. 'You have to work on those door-knocking skills.'

Gemma was still standing, staring. A frown worked its way across her face.

'What's up, sweetheart?' Mark sat up and patted the bed. 'Come here, then, and show me the cartoons.'

Claire could see her daughter was trying to work something out, and then the conversation in the car a few days before dropped into her mind.

'*But mummies and daddies sleep in the same bed!*'

'*Only if they are married.*'

'Did you get married without me?' Gemma asked, looking from her mother to her father and back again.

'What?' Mark exclaimed.

'I'll explain later,' Claire mumbled.

Claire sat on the edge of the bed and

scooped Gemma into her arms for a hug.

'No, we didn't get married without you, sweetie. Daddy and I were just waiting for you to bring the papers up. What's in the news today?'

The little girl contemplated her mum, slid off the bed as carefully as she could and showed them the front page.

'We're famous, Mum.' Gemma's smiling face round the edge of the tabloid publication would have been a picture if both her parents hadn't looked horrified at the headline and accompanying photograph.

Rock Star Mark Crofts Plays Happy Families With Secret Lovechild

'What the hell . . . ' Claire began to say. But as the meaning of the sentence sank in, she stopped. 'I guess it's true. We are playing happy families with a rock star.'

Mark looked at her, seriously. 'It's not entirely true. I don't think we're playing at it. I'm certainly not. Claire, I asked you once before, and now I'm asking you again. Will you marry me?'

Gemma squealed with excitement.

Claire looked from her daughter to Mark and back.

'Yes.'

Claire heard noises outside in the street. As she peeked out of the curtain, she saw photographers lining the path and filling her garden. 'So how long before we tell the masses out there?'

'They can wait. We have the cartoons to read yet,' Mark replied.

Claire jumped back onto the bed with her fiancé and their daughter to enjoy a few hours' peace before they told the world their happy news.

We do hope that you have enjoyed reading this large print book.

Did you know that all of our titles are available for purchase?

We publish a wide range of high quality large print books including:
Romances, Mysteries, Classics
General Fiction
Non Fiction and Westerns

Special interest titles available in large print are:
The Little Oxford Dictionary
Music Book, Song Book
Hymn Book, Service Book

Also available from us courtesy of Oxford University Press:
Young Readers' Dictionary
(large print edition)
Young Readers' Thesaurus
(large print edition)

For further information or a free brochure, please contact us at:
Ulverscroft Large Print Books Ltd.,
The Green, Bradgate Road, Anstey,
Leicester, LE7 7FU, England.
Tel: (00 44) **0116 236 4325**
Fax: (00 44) **0116 234 0205**

A MOST UNUSUAL CHRISTMAS

Fenella J. Miller

Cressida Hadley is delighted when Lord Bromley and his family are unexpectedly obliged to spend Christmas at her family home, the Abbey. True, Bromley's brother has a broken leg, her father and the earl have taken an instant dislike to each other, and the Dowager Lady Bromley drinks too much — but Cressida is convinced she can overcome these difficulties to arrange a merry holiday season. However, she has not taken into consideration the possibility that she might fall in love with Lord Bromley himself . . .

WHERE WE BELONG

Angela Britnell

Blamed for his sister's tragic death, estranged from his family, and his career in tatters, American Broadway singing star Liam Delaroche travels to Trelanow in Cornwall, searching for a new life. Meanwhile, local schoolteacher Ellie Teague is on a mission to establish her independence after jilting Will, her longtime fiancé. The attraction between the two is instant and electric. But the shadow of Liam's past looms over their growing relationship — and then the first of his bitter family members shows up in Trelanow . . .

THE WYLDES OF CHELLOW HALL

Eileen Knowles

1950s Yorkshire: Annabel journeys to her former workplace of Chellow Hall, home of the Wylde family. An unmarried mother, she has brought her baby Tommy — son and heir to one of the Wyldes — with her, feeling she should inform his father of the child's parentage. But disaster strikes when, near the Hall, she is knocked unconscious, waking later with amnesia. She has no memory whatsoever of her name, her reason for being there — or her son . . .

DISCOVERING LOVE

Wendy Kremer

When Kim, accounts manager for an archaeological excavation, meets Alex, the dig manager, a mutual attraction flourishes between them. But Alex's colleague Gloria is not so keen on Kim — might she have her eye on Alex for herself? Meanwhile, Kim's sister Julie — a brilliant mathematician, who flits from one boyfriend to another — appears to be falling in love with David, the rich sponsor of the dig. Is it a harmless flirtation, or will she end up with a broken heart?

THE PORTRAIT PAINTER

Beth James

Georgiana Rankin's passion has always been painting, following in the footsteps of her beloved Pa. When the opportunity to produce a family portrait of the prestigious Merryfields is offered, she takes it — hoping her past will not catch up with her. Meanwhile, Kit Merryfield, the eldest son and heir, is making his way back home after being wounded in the Peninsular War. Both he and Georgiana are in for a surprise when he arrives — for they have met before . . .

LOVE WILL FIND A WAY

Margaret Mounsdon

Bethany Burnett isn't surprised to discover her godfather Wendel holding a garden party in the snow. What does take her breath away, though, is the presence of Sam Richards, bad-boy film director. His unexplained disappearance had fuelled media speculation for weeks at the time. Now, years later, he's back and filming a costume drama at Wendel's Jacobean manor house. When Wendel volunteers Bethany's services as Sam's assistant, she fears troubled times are ahead — and it is not long before her fears are realised . . .